UP TO THE MOUNTAINS AND
DOWN TO THE COUNTRYSIDE

UP TO THE MOUNTAINS AND DOWN TO THE COUNTRYSIDE

A NOVEL

Quincy Carroll

 INKSHARES

Published by Inkshares Inc., San Francisco, California
www.inkshares.com

Edited and designed by Girl Friday Productions
www.girlfridayproductions.com
Cover design by Kathleen Lynch

ISBN-13: 9781941758458
Library of Congress Control Number: 2015939062

First edition

Printed in the United States of America

For my parents

He wanted to go to the East; and his fancy was rich with pictures of Bangkok and Shanghai, and the ports of Japan: he pictured to himself palm-trees and skies blue and hot, dark-skinned people, pagodas; the scents of the Orient intoxicated his nostrils. His heart beat with passionate desire for the beauty and the strangeness of the world.

—Somerset Maugham

If I watch the end of a day—any day—I always feel it's the end of a whole epoch.

—Paul Bowles

He stood in the waiting hall of the station, searching the crowd for a seat, the Chinese squatting among their baggage and eyeing him like children through the half-muted light of the clerestory. The air was smoke-filled and dusty and close and very hot, and as the sun set, the shadows from the muntins tracked its course overhead. He reached down and gathered his belongings. Although he did not have much, what he did had been packed in the luggage at his feet—a carryall, a trolley case, a plastic-shelled valise—and, lifting them up, he could feel the disappointments that had come to form their weight. Above him, a female voice warned the crowd against mountebanks and thieves, but he could not understand her, for the hall was loud and the speakers old, and it was all Chinese to him.

The departure board changed, and as it did, those who were seated slowly turned and raised their heads. If there was hope in their eyes for encouraging news, the foreigner could not say. He limped through the crowd with the carryall over one shoulder in the manner of a baldric and the trolley case behind him on its loose and broken wheels. The valise he carried endwise, like a duffel, at his side. He could feel them watching him as he set down his things, but by now that was common, and he paid it no mind. The split-flaps rustled, then they were hushed. He squinted to read the departures.

For two years now, he had been living in their country, in a crowded metropolis where you rarely glimpsed the sun, forgotten by his people and his people lost to him. Yet despite this estrangement from his family and his friends, he felt no greater bond of kinship among the Chinese with whom he lived. He was a man of more than sixty, gaunt and disheveled, with sparse gray whiskers surrounding his mouth and a sharp, protruding jaw that called attention to his chin. Scanning the crowd, he reached into his pocket and produced a small leather book, whereon the word PASSPORT had been printed in relief across the front. There was little money inside, but from what he could tell, it was likely to be enough. He folded the bills. Then he tucked them away at his breast.

The ticket counter was a collection of twelve separate windows, but only half of them were open. He stared at the Chinese as they pushed their way forward, importunate as refugees. Stanchions meant to inspire order did nothing of the sort. The whole scene had the look of some cattle fair, and as he thought this, he picked up his bags and moved them forward, mindful of the money in the pocket of his shirt. He rotated the carryall so that it covered his chest, then shook his head sadly in what appeared to be an expression of either patronage or grief.

By the time he arrived at the window, he had frightened a child and lost a hold on one of his bags and shouldered a man to the ground. The Chinese regarded him coldly but said nothing as he leaned up to the speak-thru. *Dao Ningyuan,* he shouted. Spittle flecked the glass.

The attendant turned at the sound of his voice and considered him briefly, as one might a tramp. She furrowed her brow, tilted her head querulously.

Ng?

Dao Ningyuan, he repeated.

Shenme difang?

Ningyuan.

Still, she did not understand him. He dug out the card that the school had sent him and slid it beneath the glass. She inspected it quickly, then snorted and passed it back.

Ningyuan, she said, but it sounded the same to him.

He waited while she went through the system, arranging his money on the counter between them. The crowd, unruly, pulsed. The departure board changed, and when next he looked back, the woman was shouting something at him through the perforated glass. Exactly what, he could not tell. She reached down and pressed a button. Static crackled to life.

Maiwan le.

Eh?

Piao dou maiwan le, she said, pointing him off to the side. *Ni zhan guoqu.*

He grimaced, wagging one finger in front of the glass. I don't think you're getting me here, hon. I want to go to Ningyuan. *Ningyuan.* He held up the card and pointed at the address. *Dao Ningyuan,* ya?

The attendant gave him an exasperated look, then called the next man forward. He tried to protest, but before he could, his place had been lost and his passport dropped, his luggage toppled over. Presently, a bus came into the station, and many of those who were seated got up and stretched and headed toward the gate, but he just stood there, glaring at the crowd like a slighted immortal, committing these acts to memory as if for some future and terrible use, lamenting in his heart of hearts the sorry ways of men.

With his back to the wall, he closed his eyes and lowered himself to the floor. The ground was covered with cigarette butts and seed hulls and something that smelled like fish, but, given the circumstances, he was too upset to care. The next bus would not arrive until the morning, and because the town of Ningyuan was inaccessible by train, he would have to spend that night in the station, alone. He had gone to great pains to learn this by reading the schedules over the front, as well as by enlisting the help of an officer who did not speak English and had balked at the task. Taking out his cigarettes, he tamped them against his thigh, then lit one and closed his eyes, inhaling deeply. The nicotine, however, did little to settle his thoughts. He was in desperate need of a job.

He smoked quickly, and when he was finished, he drew up his legs and surveyed the crowd. A mother and her child stood next to him, craning their necks up at the board, and he could hear the woman reading the names of cities out loud to the boy. *Hangzhou. Nanchang. Wuhan.* Across the aisle, several old men squatted flat-soled in sandals—their elbows on their knees and their forearms turned out—in what appeared to be a posture of either offering or defeat. The foreigner looked at them, and they at him, without smile or other acknowledgment. Frowning, he turned away.

Just then, a girl came down the aisle, clacking in heels, and seated herself behind them. She was young and pretty and dressed in white kneesocks, and the men nearby all turned when they saw her. She crossed her legs, studied her nails, crossed her legs again. The foreigner dug into his pack and lit another cigarette. For all of her beauty, there was something about her look that seemed to imply a certain warmth, which he rarely saw in others and even less so in women, and as she sorted through her clutch, he smoked and chewed on what this was. Ankles, calves, thighs. Hem of gusseted skirt. For a moment, he lost himself to prurient thought, and when the girl looked over, she caught him leering like a fool. He cursed himself, lowered his eyes, and felt his cheeks go red. Beside him, the child spoke.

Mama, kan. Laowai!

His expression clouded, and, turning to face the boy, he drew in on his cigarette and cocked a snook, but this elicited no response. The boy considered him, eyes glasslike and disbelieving, before erupting into a fit of coughs resulting from the smoke. Almost at once, his mother turned and scowled, coughing as well, then took him by the arm and led him away across the hall. The foreigner sat there, watching them go.

Please, a voice said. Don't take it personally. They are not used to Westerners.

Starting at the English, he searched his way down the wall until he came to find a girl sitting with her legs crossed atop a gingham-print bag. A rosacea birthmark spoiling her chin. She wore a white cotton shirt with the placket unbuttoned and the image of an Osmanthus tree sewn across the heart. Feigning indifference, he studied her but continued smoking. Eventually, he spoke.

I don't like it when you people call me that, is all.

The girl shrugged. He didn't mean anything by it. After all, he's just a kid.

Still. It's the tone, ya?

She nodded, sympathetically, as though she too were a foreigner in that land. You have to understand, she said. Seeing you comes as a surprise. Many Chinese, they cannot help it but to stare.

The foreigner considered this. What about you? I don't seem to be making you all that uncomfortable.

That's because I've had many foreign teachers in the past.

Oh, ya? I've gotta admit. Your English is pretty good. If I didn't know any better, I'd have to say you were a native speaker.

He expected the girl to deflect this praise in an act of self-effacement, but to his surprise, she did not. Glancing up at the departure board, she smiled instead. I took fourth place at the provincial English competition last month, she said. Hopefully, next year, I'll win.

When's that?

June.

He glanced across the aisle at the girl from before, emitting a thin line of smoke in the process. Well then, he said. Still got plenty of time.

The announcement system rang overhead, bruiting another arrival. The sounds of the station returned. After a moment, she got up and approached him, extending one hand with the palm facing down. How ladylike, he thought. My name is Bella, she said. May I ask what's yours?

Thomas, he said. Then, correcting himself: Mr. Guillard.

It's a pleasure to meet you, Mr. Guillard. She had trouble pronouncing the name. A group of travelers rose to go, and he looked to see if the girl in heels was among them. She was not. Bella sat down next to him, pointing up at the board. Where are you going? she asked.

Nowhere. Tickets are all sold out.

Oh. It is such a pity! Guillard exhaled, and as he did, Bella drew back noticeably, waving her hand between them in an effort to chase down the smoke. What are you going to do?

He shrugged.

Is there anything I can do to help?

No. Not unless you've got an extra ticket to *Ningyuan*.

At this, her countenance brightened. *Ningyuan?* she asked, in a pair of tones only slightly different than the ones he had used. I'm going there, too! Suddenly, however, her face went dim. Why do you want to go to *Ningyuan*?

I've got to see about a job.

You're a teacher?

He nodded.

Where?

Well, till recently, right here in Changsha. Yali Zhongxue. Before that, at Number Twelve.

Yali Zhongxue? It is such a great school! You must be an excellent teacher.

Guillard raised one hand, pretended to balance it like a scale. *Mamahuhu,* he said. Bella laughed.

Your Chinese is so wonderful! Why do you want to teach in *Ningyuan,* though? It is such a poor place.

Guillard coughed, shielding himself from Bella, and began to hammer away at his chest. Then he hawked and leaned and spat. Trust me, he said. It's not my decision. Yali screwed me. At this point, I'm willing to take whatever I can get. There's only two weeks left on my visa.

Are you American?

Mei cuo.

She smiled. Which state?

Minnesota.

Her eyes grew wide in recognition. The Land of Ten Thousand Lakes. She said the name carefully, as if reciting it from a book. It must be beautiful there. I had a teacher once from Minnesota. His name was Paul. Do you know him?

Guillard smiled weakly, stubbing out his cigarette. No, he said. I don't know Paul.

Oh. Well. Why don't you just go back? It is such a powerful country, and surely you must have a family there.

Guillard tried his best to conceal the pain occasioned by this remark. I like things better over here, he said. Life is more interesting. The split-flaps rustled. He gazed across the hall. There's this guy I know who told me that his brother had to leave Ningyuan last month. Apparently, he didn't give the school much of a heads-up. From what I've heard, they're still looking to find a replacement.

What was his name? Bella asked anxiously. The teacher who left.

I'm not sure. He's African—that's all I know. Anyway, it's been impossible to get in contact with the school. Can't say I'm much surprised. I'm going to have to get on the first bus out of here in the morning and hope I get there before they hire someone else. Otherwise—he looked at her—*bu hao.*

Don't worry, Mr. Thomas. Where there is a will, there is a way! Guillard eyed her obliquely and winced. She did not seem to notice. I'll help find a seat for you on my bus. Rummaging through her knapsack, she pulled out a small plastic bag—nearly bursting at the seams—and set it on the floor between them. By the way, she asked. Have you eaten dinner yet?

———

They sat together on the floor of the station, eating noodles from paper bowls. Bella told him of the town and its people and the places she had been, while Guillard listened impatiently, slurping at his food. He had already made his way through two oranges and a moon cake and an egg that had been steeped in tea, and the rinds from the fruit lay strewn about his person, like so many fallen leaves. As though he himself were deciduous in nature. Fragments of the eggshell littered his clothes, and with a contorted hand, he set down the noodles and wiped at his chin, then began to pick them individually from the surface of his chest. In time, he was able to tune out Bella, carping aloud in his head.

The others in their vicinity had all left by now, save the girl he had eyes for and a small group of Uighurs and a man who sat at the end of their aisle, scrolling through his phone. He did not have any luggage on him, nor did he appear to be waiting for someone, and as the Uighurs talked, he took a swig from his beer, then set it back down at his legs. A yellow tassel hung from the corner of his phone, swaying as he typed. Guillard picked up his noodles and dumped in the shells. He was full, and, at that, he was glad. When his focus finally returned to the conversation, Bella had not stopped talking.

It was such a coincidence, she said. Don't you think? He nodded and told her yes, even though he had no idea what she was talking about. She smiled. What about you, Mr. Thomas? Have you ever been to *Fenghuang*?

No. But I've heard of it. That's the town with the river running through it, ya?

Yes, the *Tuojiang*. But it's also the home to some minority people. In Chinese, the name means phoenix.

Hey. We've got one of those, too.

Pardon?

Phoenix. There's a city by that name in America, too.

Oh, yes. Of course. The capital of Arizona.

Wryly, Guillard smiled. You sure do know your geography, don't you?

Teacher Daniel taught us all about the states and their capitals last year. I can still name them. Would you like to hear?

Guillard leaned forward and studied the floor, picking a few of the shell shards he had missed from his lap. That's all right, he said. He was growing tired of this girl and her know-it-all comportment. She was boring and officious and ugly to boot. He attempted to change the subject. How is it you've been able to visit all of these places?

Bella pouted, and in that moment he realized that she must have just been telling him. My auntie and uncle, she said. They have very much money. Every summer holiday, we go traveling together: *Beijing, Shanghai, Xi'an*, Hong Kong. This year, they took me to *Wulingyuan. Zhangjiajie.* Do you know it?

Of course, he lied.

It's beautiful, yes?

You bet. Guillard sat there, examining her birthmark, trying to figure out which of the fifty states it resembled most. What about your parents? he asked. Where are they?

Mr. *Thomas* . . .

At this, the Uighurs sitting across the aisle from them started from what they were saying, disgruntled and vaguely alarmed, then eventually returned to their conversation. They are working in *Guangzhou*, she said. Remember? She studied him for a moment, as though he were senile, rubbing her chin. Pennsylvania, he thought. No, more like Iowa. Is everything all right?

Guillard frowned. He still had several questions, but he kept them to himself. Like who was this Teacher Daniel? Were there any other foreigners in Ningyuan? He had been given the impression that this was a dirty backwater town. He had not been expecting the prospect of company. Rearranging his luggage, he started to get up. Watch my stuff for a minute, he said. I need to take a leak.

Bella looked at him. A leak?

WC.

Oh, she said, shyly. I know.

The lavatory was located directly across the hall, but he took the long way around to avoid passing the girl. She had been watching him while he talked to Bella, and he had been watching her too, although strictly out of the corner of one eye, like a boy at school. She smiled at him now as he went down the aisle, his flail arm suspended and his bad leg in tow. Vendors sat perched like birds in their stalls, watching him as he passed.

He purchased a new pack of cigarettes after trying to bargain down the price, but the man he bought them from was humorless, suggesting initially that he look someplace else. In front of the lavatory, there was a woman charging admission by the door, and her coarse woolen jacket made her appear larger than she was. She gave Guillard a package of tissues and eyed him warily as she counted his change, then watched as he pushed his way past her into the washroom, negotiating the puddles of water and phlegm and vomit that lay exposed about the floor. A heady smell of excrement flooded his nose. Several of the locals squatted idly in the darkness, like panners over their stools. Toadish sounds of flatulence issued from the wall.

Finding a place in front of the tiling, he felt his bladder begin to work, and as he stood there making water, the girl reentered his thoughts. She had been flirting with him—that much was certain—and, what's more, she had been hot. By that point, Guillard had come to recognize the facial subtleties of the Chinese by heart: admiration, bewilderment, circumspection—sometimes, fear. The status they afforded him in their country was one of the few points of merit he was willing to acknowledge in their favor. That and a certain freedom: a disconnection from his past.

Once he was finished, he returned to the washroom and held his hands beneath the sink, shaking them out like rags in the darkness, wiping them down his pants. A large crack ran down the face of the mirror with dried bits of sputum on the glass, and as he stood there inspecting his image, he searched for features, not faults. He was a runt of a human being with little kindness on his face, and even though his cheekbones suggested a hardness that often appealed to the opposite sex, he could no longer bear with any favor the image opposed to him. Removing his glasses, he cleaned them with water—baring his teeth, combing his hair—then made for the exit, hobbling slightly, his forearms leading the way.

Please, a bystander muttered. But he was not seeking alms. He held out a phone to Guillard in the darkness, its screen lit by the naked picture of an underage girl. She stood milking a hard piece of candy, its handle protruding between her lips, her bra unfastened and parted like curtains, her tiny chest exposed. Guillard attempted to brush past the man, withdrawing his hand in a look of disgust, but the pimp was faster and countered to block him, not so easily discouraged. They shuffled back and forth in this manner, as if engaged in some odd form of dance, their tempo arrhythmic and shambling, the footwork of the drunk. The lighting was stronger in the doorway, but still Guillard could not see who it was. Eventually, his eyes adjusted. He noticed the tassel from before.

Beautiful, the pimp said. He elongated each syllable, as if uncertain of the sounds. With an effeminate thumbnail, he browsed through the roll, tapping the screen at points for emphasis, quoting prices with his hand. The girls had numbers to go with their photos, and they all had extremely large eyes, but there was a sadness to them also, and in this way—more than any other—they were the same.

Bu yao, Guillard said, pushing his way back out into the hall. The concourse was crowded with incoming travelers. He could smell their bodies on the air. He limped back to where Bella sat, taking the same route as before, the man from whom he had purchased his cigarettes earlier smiling broadly now, flirting with a couple of women who spoke in rapid Changshahua. Bella was exactly where he had left her, encamped among their bags, and when she saw him, she started waving, as though his return was somehow surprising to her, or he had been away for too long.

———

The boy standing in front of Guillard had to be either deaf or partway retarded. He held up a sign in one hand and in the other a metal hanger, from which an assortment of gewgaws dangled and spun. Rabbit's feet. Fuwa dolls. Commemorative portraits of Mao. The other passengers had already boarded, even though, according to Bella, it would still be some time until they left. Growing impatient, the boy grunted and pointed and held up his sign. Then he grunted and pointed again. Guillard peered at the characters, shaking his head. *Kan bu dong,* he told him.

The station they were at serviced all lines running south, and from the departure bays out back, you could see into the distance, where the sky above the horizon held but a few last colors yet. Apartment buildings loomed in profile, their floors untenanted in the dusk, banners draped to promote their developers hung with several upside-down eights. The lot was filled with empty vehicles, even though most of them were only there for one night, while up and down the aisles, mangy dogs with spotted pelts went trotting, pissing on the tanks. The boy made a face at Guillard, attempting to read what he had said, but if he was able to gather anything there from the movement of his lips, it did not discourage him. He grunted and pointed again. Guillard gave up on trying to board and shuffled off. He fell to eavesdropping on Bella, who stood arguing with the bus driver, lobbying on his behalf.

It was nearly seven thirty, but they were supposed to have left by six. Guillard had spent his time playing cards inside of the station, and even though he had put away three beers in the process, he was still a ways from being drunk. He had started with a game of Canfield, ignoring Bella for as long as he could, the girl begging him to explain the rules to her so she could help him, as, by that point, it had been clear that he needed help. The Chinese were incurable kibitzers, and so, in the end, Guillard had decided to save himself the trouble and let her teach him something else, a trick-taking variation on poker, which, according to her, was one of the most popular games in China. Unfortunately, it required three people, and this she had not thought to mention until the end. Guillard had looked at her, shaking his head, then sighed and folded his hand.

The driver of the bus seemed equally sore at her now, loading the hold while she badgered him playfully, the other passengers observing them—as was customary in that province—with lifeless expressions of interest behind the glass. He listened to them talk. The driver, crouched at his work, was barely contributing to the conversation. Out in the lot, a group of delinquents was hunting up bottles to smash and shy at the dogs. Guillard was of half a mind to lecture them, but in the end he did not, for, at that moment, the girl from earlier came out and smiled at him and seated herself on a bench.

She was skinnier than he had taken her for. Small wrists, small neck. Through her shirt, he could see her bra—a black, shoulder-less wraparound that held her tits in check. He deliberated whether or not to go over to her, groping at possible translations of things he might say in the back of his head. She took out her cigarettes and began to look for a lighter, but as luck would have it, she had none. Frowning, she bit down on the filter, like a spoiled little brat. It was then, for the first time, Guillard noticed she had braces.

Dao Ningyuan ma? he asked, offering her his matches. The girl studied him shyly, then blushed and shook her head. He stood pointing at the bus. Stickers had been applied over the windshield, stating destination and point of origin, and although he recognized the characters for Changsha, the ones for Ningyuan were still new to him. He sat down on the bench. *Dao nali a?* he asked.

The girl was bashful and would not tell him, but she sounded excited, giving him hope. She asked where he was from, and Guillard made a joke he often used about being 100 percent manufactured in the U.S. She did not seem to get it. Pointing at another bus, he asked her again where she was going, but again she would not tell him, and he felt his confidence begin to wane. She said something Guillard did not understand, but he nodded and pretended to follow along anyway. She grew silent and sat there, as if waiting for him to respond. At this point, he realized that she must have just asked him a question.

Shenme?

She laughed, holding a hand over her mouth, as if what he had said were indecent. The peddler came by, running his fingers down the hanger and setting the items there into motion, like a dull collection of chimes. The girl browsed out of courtesy, but it was clear that she was not interested. By the time Guillard had shooed the boy off, the bus had fired up.

The girl finished her cigarette. Guillard offered her another, cupping his hands to protect the flame, then pocketed the matches. Bella was walking over to them now, but he could not read her expression in the darkness. Behind her, a pair of dogs rolled in the distance, raising a pale, ocherous dust.

Good news, Mr. Thomas! The driver has agreed to take you on. She glanced at the girl sitting next to him and frowned. You must pay now, though. He did not like the idea of you paying once we get to *Ningyuan*.

Guillard pulled out his money and began to sort through the bills. They were foul due to the humidity, much like the bearer himself. Did you explain what's going on? This is all I've got. Really. The school will be good for the rest of it, though. Tell him there's no need to worry, ya?

Like a bookmaker, Bella riffled through the money. Then she counted it a second time, shaking her head.

This is not enough.

How short are we?

She worked on the translation. When the meaning dawned on her, she smiled.

Forty *kuai*.

Guillard snorted. What is that, like six or seven bucks?

Yes. Approximately.

And that's gonna be the difference? Seriously?

I'm afraid so. He is quite stubborn, I think. She looked down at her feet, scuffed a pebble with her toe. I can borrow it to you, she said, but I will need it back by tomorrow. It's my money for school.

Guillard laughed. He sat up, stretching his arms overhead, then set them down on the back of the bench. The girl next to him shifted nervously, but other than that, she did not seem to object. And here I was wondering what the hell I was gonna do, he said. You should mention things like that earlier next time, ya?

Sorry.

No. Thank you. You're saving my butt.

It's nothing.

Guillard smiled. Unheeling one of his feet from an openwork sandal, he began to scratch down the length of his calf. And it's lend, he said. Not borrow. You can lend me the money. I'm the one who's going to borrow it.

Oh, yes, Bella said. Thank you, Mr. Thomas.

How much longer till we leave?

A few more minutes, but we should get on the bus to find seats.

Guillard cocked his head toward the girl sitting next to him. Save one for me, ya? We're kind of in the middle of something.

But Mr. Thomas . . .

Guillard glared at her, flapping one hand at the bus. Bella lowered her head, then raised it again, piercing the girl with a jealous, hateful stare. Perhaps she's something of a woman yet, he thought. He followed her with his eyes as she boarded the bus, but he was not satisfied by her departure until she had taken her seat. Apologizing to the girl, he tried to resume where they had left off.

They conversed in stilted Chinese, the girl leading him as best she could, Guillard trying his best to keep up despite the nonstandard nature of her pronunciation. She came from somewhere in Hubei Province and had just turned twenty-four that year, and even though she had studied English for a few years in school, she could mumble no more than a handful of words. Guillard told her of his troubles, but somehow it seemed like he was talking about someone else, and as he continued, the girl nodded in complete fascination, her braces humped against her lips.

The driver had loaded the last of their bags, and he was now yelling at Guillard to board. The bus was weathered by the roads it had been down, the roads that lay ahead. As Guillard rose, he lifted his arms, as if to say that this was it, and for a moment they stared at each other—fondly?—the engine humming behind him. The girl blushed and broke her gaze, then asked whether he really had to go. Guillard nodded and, without another word, limped his way over and onto the bus.

Bella was seated in the back, but there were five other passengers in the aisle, and they had to file off before he could get to her, plastic footstools in hand. The cabin was hot, and it smelled of areca nuts—a menthol-like odor that hung in the air—and when he got back on board, he noticed that all of the seats were gone. A green stool sat waiting for him. Guillard stood over it and frowned. He grunted in disapproval.

What's this?

Your seat, Bella said. I'm sorry, Mr. Thomas, but there were only a few chairs left when I got on. I couldn't find any that were next to each other.

Who said we had to sit together?

I don't know. I thought you might have wanted to talk.

Guillard stowed his carryall, then looked at the stool, kicking it with his foot. I'm not sitting here, he said. My back would give out before we even made it to Zhuzhou. He looked around the cabin. The others in the aisle had returned to their positions, effectively trapping him where he stood, while up front, a few clouds of smoke had begun to appear, like monitory signals, above the chairs. A baby was crying. At the top of the stairs, a man stood with a shoulderful of farming equipment, resignedly scanning the length of the bus. I don't suppose anyone's gonna give up their seat for me, Guillard said, ya?

He lowered his body dramatically onto the stool and dragged his bad leg back and forth, like that of an awkward marionette. The woman in front of him turned around and shot him daggers with her eyes, but when it came down to it, she did not say anything. Guillard hunched forward, bowing his head. He gathered his hands in his lap. The engine was running beneath the floorboards and sending vibrations up his back, but they had not moved a single inch since he had boarded. Suddenly, it cut out. He groaned and looked up toward the front. The driver was standing in the stairwell, screaming into the lot.

He could tell that Bella was watching him, but he paid her no mind. He sat there, cursing his luck. Just as he felt himself on the verge of fading off, she tapped him on the shoulder.

Mr. Thomas?

What.

Are you awake?

No.

Sorry, she said. I didn't mean to wake you.

Impatiently, he groaned. *Shuo.*

She hesitated for a moment. Do you want to change seats?

He let out a sigh of relief. Sitting up, he smiled at her. I thought you'd never ask.

They made the switch in silence, settling back down into their thoughts. Her seat was better but still uncomfortable, and it took him a minute to learn how to sit. Through the window, he could see the dogs still fighting out in the lot, the lights of other buses against the station, the purser with her manifest, the girl on the bench. In the time since he had left her, she had attracted the attention of someone else, and they were sitting next to each other, chatting, the girl toying with her hair. She seemed more confident than before, no longer looking downward when addressed, but eventually he came to realize that they were fighting, shouting back and forth. Rising, the man struck her, and, briefly, his face flashed in the light, and for the second time that day, it was an unwelcome sight. The girl sat there, shell-shocked, clutching her cheek. The driver reboarded and started the bus, waking those who had fallen asleep, and as they backed out into the road, Guillard sat there, watching the scene through the window like an apathetic ghost. He felt no sympathy for the girl, only pity for himself.

一

二

The next morning, on the far side of town, a young man came up one of the ramps from the riverside market, carrying a brace of fowl at his hip and a rusty cleaver in the hand opposite, like some brutish old woodsman, returning at dawn. The men he passed smiled in acknowledgment, studying his arms, while vendors clamored hoarsely on the landing down below, where they had installed themselves in aisles and arranged their produce for display and terrified rabbits quivered on tables with dilated pupils and no legs. Crossing the bridge toward the square, Daniel breathed the morning air. The smell was familiar to him—raw. It felt good to be home.

He had been back for several weeks now, enjoying the summer as best he could. Ningyuan had changed in the month he had been gone, and there seemed to be no end to the development in sight. One side of the plaza was bordered by a Confucian temple that had made it through the Cultural Revolution unscathed, but everywhere else the buildings were new to him or, if not, pending renovation. A group of old men had gathered in front of one of the ates to stand and watch the machines at work. Above them, the boom of a crane hung poised like a rifle, pointing west.

He followed its line and stared off over the horizon and thought back to the month he had spent in the States. It had been good to see his family, but other than that, it had been a wash. His parents had moved into the city, and they lived a very different life now, and although he knew he would always be welcome, for some reason, it did not feel like home. Sleeping in a bed he did not deserve. Eating out at restaurants he never would have been able to afford on his own. It had been stranger to him than when he had first moved to China, and that he had not been expecting.

He had also seen his friends, but nothing much about them had changed. He could feel their bonds beginning to fade. They had talked him into going out with them his first night back in town, but, as always, Daniel had just ended up drinking too much and going home early from the bars. They asked him about China, but he could not articulate how it had changed him, for, despite trying his hardest, he could not explain it to himself. There was a wildness to the country that fulfilled certain promises in his heart, promises he had made to himself as a boy but had long since forgotten. His friends were lawyers and bankers and doctors, and they all had extremely good hearts, but Daniel could tell that they thought it embarrassing for him to be working as a teacher.

Fording the traffic, he dropped the hens on the pavement and set to unlocking the chains on his bike. The birds bated uselessly, squirming like fish. Daniel stowed the knife inside of his backpack, then produced two lengths of rope from his pants, tying the birds individually to the pillion by their feet. After several kicks, the engine came to life. As he shifted into gear, he heard someone call his name across the square.

At first he thought it was Bella, but, to his relief, it was not. The two girls approaching him had been in one of his weaker classes the year before. He could not remember their names. They crossed the square slowly, holding hands, then turned and looked at each other shyly. They seemed less assured of themselves up close. Although it was the first day of school, they were not wearing uniforms, and right away Daniel noticed their hair—it was longer than allowed. He cut the engine and waved hello. They had on matching Union Jack T-shirts and shorts made out of denim that showed their thighs, and the pockets were so long that they hung down well past their hemlines, lolling like tongues. He asked them about their summer, then told them briefly about his, then asked if they had had any opportunities to practice their spoken English, but they only looked at him and laughed. They wanted to see his tattoos. Daniel had gotten a new one over the summer, but he would not tell them where it was, and while they searched his arms, he guided them playfully, offering hints of hot and cold. There were flowers opening and ornate paisleys and dragons and koi fish in a pond that circled each other lazily, head to tail, in a representation of the duality of all things. The bolder of the two girls traced a sunburst with her hand, until she arrived at the characters for their town—宁远—on the inside of his arm. She pointed it out to her friend, but the other girl did not appear impressed. Apparently, she thought it funny. Why you doing this? she asked.

I don't know, Daniel said. Ningyuan is important to me, I guess. I got it so I won't forget.

Ningyuan? Important?

Absolutely. You should take pride in where you're from. This town is a beautiful place.

They considered him uncertainly. Then they turned to each other and laughed.

Daniel cleared his throat. Shouldn't you two be heading off? It's quarter to eight already. You don't want to be late . . .

It does not matter, the shy one said. We are not being students anymore.

What? Why not?

We are working in the markets. If you have time, come by and visit. We give you a discount, if you like.

He passed a number of other students as he rode across town, and those he knew called out his name. A few he did not did, too. He kept an eye out for Bella, even though the chances of running into her were small, since she was a boarder at the school, but you could never be too careful, especially with her. The streets became narrower as he went. Farmers quirting cattle down the side of the road, a pink-and-white albino at the head of a cart. Middle-aged women perusing the storefronts, dressed in pajamas, shopping for food. The sidewalks were abuzz with butchers and loud-speakers set out earlier that morning by the owners of stores, and, over the noise, vendors of fruit and traveling salesmen could be heard calling after pedestrians, hawking their wares. Several of the shopkeepers waved to Daniel, and he honked, for they were friends. In time, after taking a shortcut down one of the alleys, he emerged onto the street in front of Yi Zhong.

The gate was imposing but stripped of all ornamentation, aside from a banner that spanned its width. At its base, a pair of lions stood guard, pawing the plinths underfoot. The school lay at the end of a dusty road that ran all the way from the station across town, then spilled out into the countryside rather abruptly, like the mouth of some river that had nowhere to go. Within, the school bell had begun to ring, but Daniel did not have to teach until that afternoon. Without, boys and girls dressed in identical tracksuits thronged the entrance, their hairstyles cropped in the way of recruits. Between the junior and senior schools, there was a total of more than seven thousand students, but only three foreign teachers that year. Their liaison, James Li, had yet to put forward any ideas about how they might make this work. For his part, Daniel did not want to take on any extra classes. He had been down that road before. He sped past the entrance, revving his engine, then mounted the curb to the sound of applause.

The carpenter lived across from the school where he had studied as a boy, but for his son, he had greater ambitions. He stood on the sidewalk, sanding a desk, and when he caught sight of Daniel, he removed his goggles, pulling them down around his neck. He called out for his son, who was playing inside, then flashed Daniel a toothy, artless grin.

The boy was seven years old and had therefore yet to enroll at Yi Zhong, but his English was better than half of Daniel's students. He came charging out of the back. He was thin as a rail and slightly robotic, formulating every sentence inside of his head, and whenever the three of them got together, he ended up doing most of the talking. His English name was Daniel. Daniel had given him this name the year before, at his request, on a night when his parents had invited all of the foreign teachers over for dinner—something the family did a lot. Not only had Daniel eaten his last meal with them before departing, but they had also been the first people to invite him over once he was back. They stored his motorcycle for him inside their house, since even the campus had proven unsafe, and supplied him with lumber whenever he needed it. All he had to do was ask.

He spoke with the boy and gave him some old movies that he had been promising him for weeks. After looking them over, the boy asked his father if he could watch them, tugging at his belt. Always unable to refuse him, the carpenter nodded and watched him dart back inside, then took out a pack of cigarettes from the carton Daniel had given him and handed one across.

They smoked and talked about the weather. Daniel tried to keep up. The carpenter spoke in the local dialect, which was not very similar to Mandarin, but he was patient and did not mind explaining things to Daniel when it was clear that he was lost. Daniel told him about a new project he was planning and unfolded a set of blueprints he had designed himself, the angles drawn in meticulous detail, the measurements written in Chinese. The carpenter studied the plans carefully, for they were more complex than the others he had seen, then asked Daniel what it was he was supposed to be looking at, and when the boy told him, he laughed. There was a pile of wood inside the doorway next to the band saw, and with permission, Daniel went through it, picking out the pieces that he liked. Lashing them to the back of his motorcycle, he thanked the man. Then he was off.

The gate was no longer crowded, and as Daniel rode underneath the propaganda strung overhead, the guards hailed him, waving their arms, instructing him to stop. They too were smoking a brand of cigarette he had brought back with him from the States, and they too offered him one when he pulled up, fumbling for a light. The school was looking for him, they said. Mrs. Ou had left a message. His residence permit had been approved, and he could pick it up whenever he liked. One of his students had been by as well, and from the description they gave, he could tell they were talking about Bella. He told them he would be sure to head over to the office once he had unloaded his bike, and the guards seemed satisfied by this, retaking their seats. His building was on the far side of campus, and by the time he got there, the cigarette they had given him had burned down to ashes, drooping from his lips.

He lived on the top floor of the dormitory, and the lumber alone took him several trips. He peered in through the doorways that had been left open, his neighbors nodding as he passed. A woman preceded him on the stairs, delivering food from across the street, and on his way back down, she was there again, but Daniel kept his distance so as not to crowd her, out of respect. A note had been taped to his door, but as he was fairly certain whom it was from, he did not hurry himself to read it. He hauled the wood up to the roof. He penned the chickens in a coop he had built on the balcony the day before, then took down his laundry from the clothesline and folded it neatly or, at least, the best he could. Finally, he remembered the letter. It had been written on purple stationery with pictures of Hello Kitty on the front, and it had been folded in half twice to keep the contents safe. The tape Bella had used had left a mark on his door.

For someone who spoke so well, she had trouble writing in English. There were errors in syntax and misgendered pronouns and, at one point, words in Chinese. The dots over certain letters drawn like hearts. He read about her trip to Wulingyuan with her aunt and uncle the previous month as well as how she had met a man in the capital who came from Minnesota. His name was Thomas. He was a decorated war hero—apparently a real mensch from the sound of it—and according to Bella, he was "very interesting," although he would never compare to Daniel. He was looking for a job, and, using her English, she had been able to help him, but any credit for this belonged to her teacher, for without his instruction, she would have been lost. Anyway, the note finished, as of last night, she was back! She was excited to meet the new foreign teachers—when could they all hang out? Shaking his head, Daniel crumpled up the letter, then tossed it into the trash. Incorrigible, he thought—that was the word.

———

Midday found him on the roof, eating a bowl of noodles he had cooked himself, the students at play below in the yard, the campus alive with the sound of their shouts. He still had an hour and a half left before he had to get to class, and, besides, the weather was beautiful. He opened another beer. The river wended past the courts, the mountains rising in the distance, and from where he sat, Daniel had an unobstructed view of everything the countryside had to offer. In his mind, Ningyuan was a charming, idyllic place. Behind him, the roof was scattered with tools and wood and trash from the times he had invited his friends up to eat with him that month as well as a few rattan chairs and a pane of glass that had been set between them on a pair of empty jugs. He had drawn up the ladder so that no one would follow him and covered the hatch with corrugated tin, using a brick to hold it down. As he ate, he watched the students. He envied them slightly. Although they did not know it at the moment, they were the ones who had it good.

He had spent most of that morning sawing down the lumber and then stacking the pieces for future use. The sun had burned him in the process, but fortunately his hair had saved his neck. He had grown it out over the summer and dyed it red upon return, and he had to say, he rather liked it—not as bright as he had been expecting. The Chinese gaped at him in the streets, but even without it that would have been the case. After two weeks, however, they seemed to have grown used to it. Ningyuan was not such a big place.

He finished his noodles and then the beer and then prepared to climb back down. A group of boys was playing basketball in front of the river, and when he stood up, they saw him. One waved. Daniel saluted, raising his bowl. Not a single court was empty. A few girls were playing badminton and running in circles around the track, and there were blankets laid out on top of the exercise equipment, drying in the sun. Along the riverbank, a pile of trash smoldered lightly. Turning, Daniel suddenly caught sight of a man limping across the courts. One of his shoulders was cocked at the ear, and, whether out of pity or derision, the students all whispered as he passed. He moved awkwardly, traversing the schoolyard, disrupting several games to the point of stopping, and as he did, two boys approached him, but he did not receive them, just waved them off. Lowering himself into a squat, Daniel observed the man from his perch. Mr. Thomas—it had to be. He was headed toward the office with a train of followers in his wake, the kids stalking him at a distance, one teacher pointing while he held his books. The office. Daniel had completely forgotten. He watched the man round the corner of the building, then uncovered the hatch and lowered the ladder. James Li had been holding his passport now for two weeks. The less time he had it, the better.

He took the same path as the old man across the yard, carrying a box of books he had received that morning. He had founded an English library above the office the year before and recruited his friends and relatives to send him donations. So far, however, the results had been disappointing. This batch had come from his mother. Still, the room was his, and it stayed cool during hot weather, and when it rained, he held English Corner there. On Sundays, all were welcome. He had a vision for what the place could be. It just needed a little work.

The other rooms on the floor were inhabited by teachers, but Daniel did not know them. Washing hung in the hall. He had painted the door with his students, and over the lintel, there was a sign made out of wood that read NINGYUAN YI ZHONG ENGLISH LIBRARY. He tried his key, but it did not fit. At first, Daniel thought he had selected the wrong one, but after flipping through the rest of them, he realized that the lock had been changed. Typical, he thought. He shook the door, but no one answered.

Plodding back downstairs. From the office, he could hear an argument underway. A voice he did not recognize was shouting something in Chinese, but it had to belong to the foreigner, for his Chinese was atrocious. James Li was trying to talk him down, but from the sound of it, he was not getting very far. When Daniel knocked, everyone in the room looked up. As usual, Mr. Cai, one of James's assistants, was drunk.

The foreigner was old and severely crippled, and he had a mistrustful look about him. He was wearing a button-down that was not quite Hawaiian but, given how tacky it was, might as well have been. When he saw Daniel, he exhaled. Can you help me out and talk to this guy? he said.

Before Daniel could say anything, James Li began to shout. There was nothing he could do, he said. He was sorry, but it was too late. The foreigner threw up his arms and started yelling at him, again in that terrible Chinese, and soon it seemed as if the two of them had forgotten him, so absorbed as they were in the fight. Mrs. Ou stood up to greet him. Daniel gave her a hug, which caused her to laugh.

She was a kindly woman. She handed him his passport, then poured him a cup of water and told him to sit. Her hair was drawn back tautly into a bun, and this gave her an unfortunate, narrow-eyed expression. I thought you were coming this morning, she said. I waited for over two hours!

Sorry, Mrs. Ou. I meant to, but I forgot. He flipped open his passport and checked that everything was in order. The new residence permit was there, but he looked so young in the picture. The booklet was filled with extra pages. What happened to the lock on the door upstairs?

Oh, we had to change it for another. There was no key here when you left!

Why did you have to go in?

Very danger, Mr. Cai interjected. He had stumbled over from where James Li and the foreigner stood fighting. He leaned in and narrowed his eyes, then he sniffed Daniel's breath. Almost at once, his eyes lit up. You are drunk! he said.

Daniel ignored him. Craning his neck at the other foreigner, he lowered his voice.

Who's that?

Mrs. Ou turned and looked right at the man. That is Thomas, she said. He came in very late last night.

What's going on?

He wants to teach here at *Yi Zhong*. We have told him, however, that the semester has already begun. Class rosters are set. It is too difficult to change the schedule. There is nothing we can do.

The first part was true, but Daniel knew they were just being lazy. Standing up, he walked over to the desk. James Li and the other foreigner stopped shouting and regarded him cautiously as he approached.

What's with this guy? the American asked. I swear, I'm on the verge of giving up.

His manners did him no favors, but Daniel knew how hard it could be. In his best Chinese, he reiterated how badly they needed another teacher, but James Li was stubborn and would not listen. He sat there stewing, shaking his head.

It is impossible. I have told him. There is simply nothing that we can do.

That's a lie, and you—

Well, Daniel said. That's fine. But he's come so far. Don't you think we should at least invite him to dinner?

Thomas did not understand and continued complaining as Daniel arranged it. The truth was that, by now, James Li and the others were not going to do anything. Their only hope was the principal. He was hosting a banquet that evening at the International Hotel in honor of the new foreign teachers, and if they could convince him of the idea there, he might make a direct hire. Daniel tried explaining this to the man as he herded him out the door, but Guillard just stood there, eyeing him sullenly, like a child who knows he has done wrong.

China, he finally said. Name's Thomas. You smoke?

三

The principal of the Ningyuan No. 1 Middle School was a short man, surnamed Feng, who did not speak a word of English and arrived at the banquet hall late, after all of the food had gone cold. Seated next to James Li, he welcomed the foreigners, asking them their names, then gave a speech in the local dialect that seemed to drag on forever. He wore a thick set of glasses as well as a Rolex cut from steel, bordered tastelessly with Evcrose around the wrist and on the dial, and while he talked, he eyed the waitress, a girl of no more than twenty. She had on a *qipao*, stitched with lilies, and, Jesus Christ, did she have legs, the slit running up past the middle of her thigh and leaving much to Guillard's imagination. When Feng finished his remarks, he sat down. The others applauded, but only out of courtesy. Thinking dinner had been served, Guillard picked up his chopsticks, then made for the Susan. As he did, however, James Li interrupted him, inviting the boy, who was named Daniel, to speak.

He was a strange-looking kid. His hair was red and longer than Imogen's, the girl from Canada on his left, and although he was handsome, it was hard to tell this, given the things he had done.

His arms were tattooed, top to bottom, and both of his ears had been gauged with disks, yet somehow the Chinese appeared to like him, calling him by name as he stood. He had changed into shirt-sleeves since that afternoon—a secondhand oxford, loose at the neck—and, in fact, everyone there, with the exception of Guillard, had taken the time to dress up.

His Chinese was excellent. He began by thanking James Li, Mrs. Ou, and the principal, then moved on to welcoming the new volunteers, speaking, if not with confidence, then with ease, a complete mastery of the tones. His pronunciation—at least to Guillard's ears—was better than Feng's, and by the fifth or sixth sentence, he had lost him. The Canadians, too. For their sake, James Li resumed translating. Whether due to laziness or inept-itude, his versions were much shorter, as though all that mattered was making it seem like you knew, getting the gist of it across. Suddenly everyone started laughing. Unable to offer a translation, James Li just sat there, embarrassed, and smiled. Guillard looked up, and to his annoyance, the boy was pointing at him.

The table stood and drank a glass together, two of the Chinese already drunk, the men taking spirits, the women juice, steins of tea half-filled, untouched. Prior to the toast, Daniel said some-thing that rhymed, and this was met with cheering from his col-leagues as well as plaudits from their host. The other Canadian, a man in his early thirties, started coughing from the liquor, and the Chinese laughed at him, but all in good fun. Then they sat down. Without another word, they dug in.

The Canadian's name was Christopher. He had a solemn cast about him, and he did not talk much. He and Imogen had come as a couple, but at the moment it seemed as though they were fight-ing. Once he had stopped coughing, he turned and motioned for a napkin, then wiped his mouth. Stifling a belch. With a confused expression, he turned and gaped at Guillard.

What was that?

Baijiu. Guillard smirked. Literally: white alcohol. It's a kind of liquor, made from rice.

Well, it literally tastes like vomit.

Guillard shrugged. I've had worse.

Than that?

The trick is to breathe through your mouth.

Christopher nodded. Popping open his tableware, he junked the plastic under his chair, like a moviegoer, emboldened by the dark. He did not seem to be further interested in talking, but that did not bother Guillard. This way, he could steer the conversation.

First time in China?

The man tilted his head at his girlfriend. Still our first month.

How do you like it?

Can't complain. Everything's still new.

Guillard snorted and rotated the Susan, the others picking at it as he did. The food was oily and seasoned with peppers, and there were bones in the meat. He looked over at the principal, but he was still busy talking to Daniel, calling him handsome, in the way of strangers, offering him cigarettes from a pack. Earlier, on their way over to the hotel, the boy had insisted that Guillard wait a while before bringing up the matter of employment, but that seemed pointless to him now. Guillard knew how these things worked. He had to find a way to engage the principal. At the moment, there was none.

What about you? Christopher asked.

What?

How long have you been living here?

In China? Two years.

And you like it?

Occasionally. Ya?

Christopher nodded, but he did not laugh. Any advice for a couple of newcomers?

Well, Guillard said, leveling his fist at the booze. For starters, I'd stay away from that.

There it was—a grin. Tight-lipped and barely noticeable, but a smile nonetheless. Anything else?

I could go on forever.

That bad, huh?

Guillard shrugged. What made you want to come to Asia?

Well, actually, India was our first choice, but there wasn't enough funding for the program. We'd already submitted our deposit and committed to the move, so we figured, what the hell, why not? China's close. This was the last site with any vacancies, though. We had been hoping to live in the city.

Guillard laughed, picking at his plate. He glanced over at Feng, but the boy was still monopolizing him, telling a story—half in English—about the beauty of Ningyuan. Imogen sat next to him, listening, barely touching her food, and whenever the principal addressed her, he called her beautiful. *Meinü.* She was pretty, Guillard supposed, but only in a blowsy sort of way. Christopher, on the other hand, was fastidious. You could tell by the way he ate.

What's so funny? he asked.

India, Guillard said. Probably the only country in the world that's uncleanlier than here. I'd say you lucked out. Removing his cigarettes from his shirt, he lit one, then blew smoke across the food. Somewhat hesitantly, he offered one to the Canadian. Christopher smiled. No thanks, he said. I'm actually in training for a marathon.

In addition to the principal, there were three new faces at the table: Jerry, the vice principal, a teacher from Gao Er, and a man named Connie, who, upon sitting down next to Guillard, had told him in English, rather loudly, that he could drink like a fish. Slurred though his speech was, his tolerance was admirable, for he had been drinking since they got there and, half an hour later, showed no signs of letting up. He went around the table, toasting the foreigners one by one, spelling the principal when required, goading the rest. His face had turned red from the alcohol, as though he had been left out in the sun for too long. Christopher and the teacher from Gao Er eventually bowed out of the drinking, and although Guillard had been hoping to pitch himself to the principal first, with the alcohol there in front of him, that felt like a waste. Connie toasted him a third time, spilling baijiu on his lap. This repeated itself several times, until, before he knew it, he was drunk.

There was a lull in the principal's conversation with the others, and as soon as he noticed it, Guillard picked up his glass. He thanked Feng in his best Chinese for including him at the meal. James Li murmured something to Feng—the principal smiling, nodding along—telling him how Guillard had been a teacher at Yali Zhongxue the year before in Changsha. The other Chinese regarded him, clearly impressed, the table strewn with their bones, but they did not dare to outshine the principal by expressing their thoughts on the matter first. Feng pushed back his chair and raised his glass, then nodded to Connie, who drank in his place. Rather abruptly, he called the waitress, who stood attending them next to the sideboard like a medieval courtesan, awaiting instruction.

Yali Zhongxue, Daniel said as they retook their seats. I thought they only hired their teachers through Yale.

Some, Guillard grunted. Not all. There's an international department, too. Mostly French and German, but they reserve a few spots for English as well.

The only reason I ask is that I've got a friend who used to work there. His name is Neil. Still lives in Changsha. You ever meet him?

Guillard hated this game. Sounds familiar, he said, but no. Believe it or not, there are a lot of foreigners in Changsha.

British Neil? Imogen asked. I almost forgot. Chris and I met him one night during orientation. When we told him that we had been assigned to Ningyuan, he told us that he knew you.

Daniel grinned. That's him, all right. I swear, Neil finds a way to meet everyone.

He's an . . . interesting guy. By the way Imogen said this, Guillard could tell she did not find him interesting at all. Just then, a group of men in business suits came over from one of the neighboring tables, and after Daniel answered their questions about why they were there and where they were from, the foreigners drank with them, showing them their glasses when they were done. Only the Canadians' were still full. Feng was still chatting with the waitress. Since Guillard's speech, he did not seem to be paying him any mind.

Daniel resumed where they had left off. Neil's a character— that's for sure. After Yali, he's been working on a few start-ups, but none of them have been very successful. Still, I admire the guy. He's out there, trying to make it happen, you know? Most people wouldn't have the guts. He's an entrepreneur at heart.

Imogen frowned. He seemed more like a hustler to me.

You may be right, Daniel laughed.

What about you? Guillard asked. What were you doing before China?

Living and working in New York.

Ya? Where at?

Well. It's complicated. I quit my first job only a few weeks after starting. Finance. Wasn't for me. I went into it for all of the wrong reasons. It felt like I was standing at the end of a diving board— thing is, there wasn't any water in the pool. I don't know. Maybe I'm just making excuses. I was scared, I guess. In hindsight, I think there was a reason for it, though. Once I got over that initial fear, it didn't take me long to figure out what it was I really wanted to do.

Good for you, said Imogen. Out of the corner of his eye, Guillard could see James Li nodding, too.

What was that? he asked.

Well . . . China. I worked as a waiter in a restaurant for a while, just to get by, but I studied Mandarin in college, so at the time it seemed like a good idea.

Imogen looked at him skeptically. Neil told us that you requested this placement. Is that true?

Yup. And it hasn't disappointed me. I love it here.

Really? asked Guillard.

Really.

Why in God's name would you want to live here?

The boy flushed. To be completely honest, I wanted to get away from everything, you know? Call it a sort of return to simple living. If you can believe it, Ningyuan means "a peaceful, far-off place." When I heard that, I was sold. It felt like fate.

Guillard sat there, laughing quietly to himself. Sure, he supposed he could forgive the boy for his youth, but to have thrown away a perfectly good career in the middle of a recession was idiotic by any account.

I heard it differently, he said. Someone told me that the Ning in Ningyuan actually means "pacified." A long time ago, this place was the site of a major insurrection. There wasn't anything peaceful about it.

Daniel set his chopsticks down on the rim of his bowl, then leaned forward—the better to see Guillard—and smiled. It was a sporting kind of look. His hair was dangling in front of his face, and this made it hard to take him seriously.

Yeah? he asked, a bit too cynically for Guillard's taste. Who told you that?

A student. We came in together on the same bus last night. She told me she knows you. Seems like you're pretty popular around these parts.

Daniel and the Canadians exchanged a knowing look, but of what, Guillard could not be certain. The boy smoothed a strand of hair behind one of his ears, then picked up his utensils and straightened in his chair and deftly began to convey peanuts from one of the dishes into his mouth. The Chinese were speaking among themselves, and Feng was flirting with the waitress, the girl blushing and feigning laughter as she poured him more beer. Guillard lit another cigarette. The ashtray in front of him looked like a boneyard of broken filters. Bottle caps. Seeds. At last, Imogen spoke.

Bella.

That's right. How'd you know?

She came to our apartment this morning to introduce herself. We had quite a bit of trouble getting her to leave. She invited us to her grandparents' house this weekend, but I told her most likely we'd be busy settling in.

Daniel nodded, then wiped his lips and turned to Guillard. Her heart's in the right place, but I wouldn't believe everything she tells you. She's been known to exaggerate and make things up at times, and, to be honest, I think she just likes showing off in front of foreigners. You gotta be firm with her about boundaries. Otherwise, she'll never leave you alone.

She didn't seem that bad. Trust me, I've had my share of Chinese stalkers in the past. Anyway, I doubt she'd lie about something like the meaning of the town's name. It's more believable than—what'd you call it again?—Never-Never Land.

Both of the Canadians looked at Daniel. He seemed to have taken the comment in stride, but there was a vein above one of his eyebrows that pulsed in reaction to the slight. Brusquely, he turned to Feng.

Feng Xiaozhang, qing wen: Ningyuan, zhe ge mingzi, shi cong nali qiyuan de?

The principal looked at the others, but they were staring at him. With great charm, he asked the waitress if she knew where the town's name came from, but all she did was blush and lower her head. He surveyed the table. *Zhe ge wenti,* he said, *haoxiang meiyou ren zhidao!*

No one knows! James Li shouted. The Chinese erupted into laughter. Daniel made a face at the Canadians and shrugged. Feng delivered the line again, and this prompted a second round of applause. For the life of him, however, Guillard could not see what was so funny.

Connie stood and raised a glass. *Wei meiyou ren zhidao ju yi bei!* Then he started pounding on the table.

He and Daniel and Guillard and even Feng himself drank to this embarrassing fact, then drank again, refilling their glasses immediately, as if all that the laughter needed was more alcohol to sustain it. Daniel choked on the second shot, but eventually he bolted it down, and, once all of the excitement had passed, the principal gave Guillard a look that seemed to imply that he was impressed. For a moment, at least to Guillard, it seemed as though he had forgotten about the boy.

❧

四

The semester began slowly, Guillard growing more familiar with the town, learning the places he needed to go in order to find beer, food, clothes. For the first time in recent memory, he had money to burn, and, compared to the volunteers, his pay was excellent. Outrageous, in fact. He watched them scrimp and save their earnings—eating at street stalls, cooking at home—while he dined at Old Tree, a western-style restaurant along the river near the square.

They were required to meet with James Li every Tuesday to turn in their lessons, and during this time, he would subject them to long-winded speeches on how to most effectively teach their kids. Half the time, he had no idea what he was talking about, and Guillard would ignore him, smoking a butt, trying to steal a glance at the papers that lay in sheaves upon his desk. The boy's were the easiest to read, for he wrote entirely in block letters—stringent and neat—while the Canadians' were often the same or, if not, copied from the book.

One of the lessons he borrowed from Daniel was called "An Introduction to American Holidays," and it ended with skits at the front of the classroom, groups of students in front of the board. Grades were awarded according to applause, even though, in truth, they did not matter, and this his students seemed to recognize, perhaps more so than he. Bella's class gave him the most trouble, constantly talking in Chinese, and, stalking up and down the aisle, he tried to scare them into listening, but they would not be cowed. The boys in the back were a surly lot—thin, acned delinquents who hid behind their books—and, at their most impertinent, trying to get them to participate felt like straying into an area on the wrong end of town. They were the last of the groups to present, and when Guillard summoned them, a wild hooting went up, for they were wearing masks, cut out of paper, their eyes like agates, hard and black.

They defiled through the chairs, assuming their places in front of the board. From where he sat in the back of the room, Guillard observed them. They looked like suspects, arraigned on some count. He quieted down the others, shouting and casting a furious eye, then made as if to judge the boys on their costumes: so half-assed—four sheets of paper, nothing else.

What's this?

Easter, one of the boys responded. He had on glasses over his mask, and from the way he shouted his answer, it was clear that he thought it a joke.

Guillard frowned. Halloween, you mean. Ya?

No. Easter! More forcefully this time. Guillard sat down and waited for some kind of explanation, but none seemed to be forthcoming. Taking off his glasses, he rubbed his nose.

By all means, then. *Kaishi.*

The boy in the glasses raised his arms and, in a booming, chthonic voice, began to shuffle down the aisle, like a member of the undead. The other students started howling, beating their desktops in approval, while the rest of the group hung back, a silent chorus but for their laughs.

He completed a circuit of the room, chanting something in Chinese throughout, then returned to his desk and took off his mask, avoiding Guillard's eyes. His partners were on the dais, bowing triumphantly in front of their peers, and the sound of applause, rowdy and unchecked, was now general throughout the room. Some of those seated in the audience had risen, calling for an encore, egging them on, while in the hall a different set of students had emerged from self-study, gathering in front of the window to see what was going on.

Bella, as always, was seated toward the front. Guillard slumped down and looked at her. His throat was hoarse, and consequently he had neither the patience nor the energy to put up with their crap. Bella eyed him and shrugged. I don't get it, he said.

Sheepishly, she turned to her desk mate—a fat, frog-eyed little girl—and laughed. He is Jesus, she said. After the resurrection.

Guillard had introduced this word to them at the start of the lesson, but still, he was shocked to hear that anyone had remembered it. He thought back to the performance in light of this new information, then stood up and adjusted his trousers, rolling his eyes at the godlessness of the Chinese. The class was far from over, but since he had prepared nothing else, he dismissed them early. The children streamed out, yelling and laughing, scraping the floor with their chairs.

The courtyard was empty aside from his class. The old oak at its center had nearly completed shedding its leaves, while the lowermost boughs hung close off the ground, so that anyone who wanted to could reach up and touch them. At the trunk, a system of supports had been constructed to keep the heavier ones from falling. Annoyed, Guillard tore at the foliage that still remained as he passed. The leaves were sere and crumbled instantly, but he did not wipe them from his hands. Out in the fields, farmers could be seen, stooped beneath the sun, carrying sheaves along the furrowed plots, tools upon their shoulders. Guillard found his cigarettes and lit one as he walked, the image of a molten sun red upon his eyes.

There was a pavilion, encased by Osmanthus trees, opposed to the Office of Foreign Affairs, and, to Guillard's dismay, a group of students had already assembled there, waving from the benches, calling his name. The base of the structure was built from stone, and there was a heavy circular table to serve as a hub, around which they convened every Monday and Tuesday, an extra-curricular forum for those who wished to develop their spoken English. Attendance was optional, but, of course, Bella was always there. She grinned at him as he climbed up the stairs. She looked frumpy in her tracksuit. A red scarf hung around her neck.

Hello, Mr. Thomas. Is Teacher Daniel coming today?

Raising one eyebrow, Guillard gave her a funny look. What day is it today?

Monday.

And when do Daniel and I teach English Corner?

Monday and Tuesday, right?

Exactly.

Sitting down on one of the benches across from her, he put out his cigarette on the rest. At the banquet to kick off the semester, Daniel had given the other foreign teachers an overview of their responsibilities—fifteen classes a week, sixty to seventy students each, dinner obligations with bigwigs and officials—but there had been no mention of English Corner. It was a common part of the job, but he had been hoping that, since he had saved the school's ass by signing on late, they would not ask him to take part in any activities outside of class. It had not been until James Li had shown him his contract—one copy in English, the other in Chinese—that he had learned about all of the extra duties he was expected to perform. For such a simple, run-down school, the language and terms were surprisingly formal: length of service and expected duties, a noncompete clause, policies on leaving the town for travel, a paragraph on the last page about sexual misconduct and the penalties for sleeping with a student. It had all been typed up by Mrs. Ou, both copies riddled with that absurdly comic punctuation used by the Chinese. Regarding English Corner, Imogen had asked that her evenings be kept free at the start of the week, and since neither Daniel nor Guillard really cared, they had set the schedule in this way. Guillard did not like teaching with the boy, but the Canadians were inseparable, and in any case, they only had to do it twice a week.

Apart from Bella, there were five other girls huddled in a pack on Guillard's left, as well as a boy with an effeminate demeanor, whose English name was Flower. As they waited for the bell to ring, they sat and asked Guillard questions, and, like a ruler holding court, he listened, answering each of them in turn. He had attended one or two English Corners at the universities in Changsha, but mainly to network or pick up girls, neither of which had met with great success. This was different. Lesson plans were expected, and, worst of all, he could not recycle any of his old ones, as James Li or Mrs. Ou would drop by every so often to join in on the discussion. What's more, Daniel's presence made him uneasy, even though, to be honest, he could not say why. They sat separately most nights, surrounded by their students, the boy's group larger and more animated, Bella laughing at his jokes.

I want to marry a foreigner, she said. Guillard had been asking them about their dreams. Her desk mate was sitting next to her, and this caused the girl to laugh. Guillard shifted uneasily when he heard this, for she seemed to be looking right at him. There is so much outside of China, she continued. I want to see it all!

By then, the bell had rung. Students were streaming across the yard. A crew from one class had assembled under the oak tree, equipped with handmade osier brooms. They began to sweep as the sun went down. Guillard looked at his watch and frowned. The boy was late, and it was his turn to lead. What about you? he asked.

Bella's desk mate did not like attention, and she shied at the question, lowering her eyes. They were curtained by thick, voluminous bangs and, given the tautness of her skin, appeared incapable of closing. I don't know, she said. Turning, she looked at Bella. Then she added something in Chinese.

Bella frowned but also nodded, her birthmark more obvious than ever in the light. Her prospects aren't good, she said. For a moment, an awkward silence set in. The only sound that of the leaves. In the courtyard, at the base of the pavilion, a student from one of his classes was pacing back and forth. He was listening to a conversation that had been recorded in English, muttering to himself.

Well, said Guillard. I wouldn't worry about that just yet.

But we have to. Don't you know what day it is today?

No. What?

Zhongqiujie. The Mid-Autumn Festival.

Really?

The girls nodded as one.

But what's that got to do with getting married? I thought it was like your version of Thanksgiving.

It is, but traditionally it's also a time for girls to pray to *Chang'e.*

Guillard was in the process of blowing his nose. Once he finished, he made a face, then stuffed the handkerchief back in his coat.

Chang-who-now?

Chang'e. The goddess of the moon. It's said that the sun and the moon are a couple. Their children are the stars. Every time the moon is full, it's—how do you say—*huaiyun.*

Pregnant?

Yes. Pregnant. It's for this reason that we associate the holiday with courtship and marriage.

So this woman, Chang'e—she pops out a kid every month?

The two girls looked at each other and laughed. No, Mr. Thomas. Of course not. *Change* is not the moon. She just lives there. Haven't you heard the story?

Guillard cast them a short-tempered look. When Bella saw that she had upset him, she lowered her gaze and blushed. He told them that he had never heard the story before, but for the first time since he had met her, Bella seemed shy—too hesitant to talk. Go on, he told her. Looking up, she brushed the hair from her face. Slowly, she began to recount.

A long time ago, there were ten suns. Their father was the king of heaven, and every day they would take turns traveling over the earth. One day, however, they decided to go together. The weather became so hot that the plants died, water disappeared, and the people began to suffer. Finally, the emperor was forced to beg the gods for help.

Guillard lifted one hand. Behind him, a small boy had sidled up onto the pavilion. Standing there like a monkey, hanging off the rail. He seemed too young to be a student, but given the way his ears were perked, it appeared as though he had been following the conversation. A squat, rough-looking man, whom Guillard assumed to be his father, stood below. He encouraged the boy to speak.

Hello.

Hello yourself.

The boy smiled and leaned closer. Do you know Teacher Daniel? he asked.

You betcha. He's late. Who's asking?

Daniel.

No, Guillard said, smiling. Not Daniel. You. What's your name? He pointed at the boy. Then he pointed at himself. Mr. Guillard, he said. You?

The boy frowned and clambered over the rail, then seated himself on the bench. I am Daniel, he repeated. Guillard could feel a familiar frustration beginning to well in the pit of his chest. Teacher Daniel and I have the same name. I was named because of him.

Guillard surveyed the circle, as if thinking himself to be the butt of some joke. Of course you are, he said. How come that doesn't surprise me?

Are you talking about *Chang'e?*

Sure are. *Ni zhi bu zhidao?*

The boy raised his eyebrows. You speak Chinese? Good! Behind them, the boy's father was expressing a similar sentiment, holding up two thumbs. Yes, he said, I know it. Here in China, everyone does. It is a very famous story, but—I don't know how to say—*you hen duo banben . . .*

There are a lot of versions, Bella said.

Really.

Suddenly, Guillard had an idea. Taking his keys out of his pocket, he tossed them to Flower. It was a poor throw, and the boy had to scramble to save them from going over the edge.

Let's play a game, he said. We'll tell the story together, OK? *Mei ge ren, liang ju.* If you don't have the keys, be quiet, ya? Flower, start us over again from the beginning.

This is a game? Bella asked.

Sure. The Storytelling Game. Now please, Flower. *Kaishi.*

By the time they got back to the point where Bella had left off, the keys had found their way back to her. She walked into the middle of the circle, clearing her throat.

The god of eastern heaven agreed to punish his sons, so he went to *Houyi*, the god of archery, and asked him to frighten them with his bow. Originally, *Houyi* did not want to hurt the suns, but when he saw how badly they had burned the earth, he changed his mind. So . . .

Two sentences, Guillard reminded her. Let someone else have a try, ya?

Bella pouted and stomped back to her seat. She handed the keys to the boy, and as Daniel got up to speak, she muttered something at him in the local dialect. The boy barely acknowledged her, however, saying only that he knew.

Houyi decided that in order to save the earth, he would have to shoot down the suns. But after he had killed nine of them, the god of eastern heaven had to beg him to stop. Otherwise, all of the world would be dark. He sat back down and smiled and passed the keys to his left.

Three sentences! Bella shouted. Guillard ignored her and turned to Flower.

Continue, he said.

Because the children is dying, the god of heaven is very mad. So he turns *Houyi* and his wife, *Chang'e*, into man.

What were they before?

Gods.

Oh, right. *Jixu.*

Guillard's keys jangled as they picked up steam. The other students were not very practiced at speaking English, and while they struggled with the language, Bella sat there impatiently, joggling her knees. Every time they made a mistake, Guillard had to stop her from interrupting.

Chang'e was very upset that she will be dying, said the first girl, so *Houyi* going to the West to find some medicine. The medicine can make them so that they will never be growing old.

Then *Houyi* is coming back, but he has many things to do. He gives the medicine to *Chang'e* but tell her must wait before eating.

One day, *Chang'e* is alone in the house. A bad man, *Pang Meng*, coming to speak with *Houyi*.

Really, he wanting is the medicine. When he sees where it is hidden, he try to kill *Chang'e*.

Because *Change* not want *Pang Meng* to have the medicine, so she eat it all, then jump out the window. But she has eaten too much, so started flying to the sky.

At this point, the keys came back to Bella's desk mate, but the girl deferred, shy as she was, and passed them on. Guillard checked his watch, then squinted across the yard. Still no sign of Daniel.

Change loved *Houyi* very much, Bella went on, and she did not want to go away, so she stopped on the moon, since it was closer to the earth than heaven. From there, she could always see *Houyi*, and he could see her, too.

The story seemed to be over. Guillard looked around the circle. So, he said, she's still up there all alone?

No, Bella said. There is a rabbit with her. Some people say that, if you look close, you can see it.

Guillard snorted. People see what they want.

Just then Daniel appeared, striding at a breakneck speed across campus, holding a stack of printouts in one hand, his beat-up guitar in the next. He was wearing a tie and a shirt and a pair of khakis that were covered in chalk, and his hair had been tied up into a ponytail, red as the color of that night. When Bella spotted him, she jumped—no longer concerned with anything else—and ran out to greet him, followed by the others. Guillard suddenly found himself sitting there, alone.

Sorry, Daniel said breathlessly as he came up the stairs. Surrounded by Guillard's students, he looked like some sort of shepherd, tending his flock. Several more had come over, intrigued by the sight of his instrument. They stood hesitantly along the rail, eyeing the foreigners and whispering in Chinese.

Where the hell have you been?

I had to run off a few copies. Daniel dropped the stack on the table, and almost at once, the sheets were gone. The children snatched them up, passing them around, reading the lyrics in pairs. The print shop was a mess, he said. They kept me waiting for nearly an hour.

They like to take their time all right. You gotta show up early.

Daniel nodded, tuning his guitar. There were stickers coating the body and a capo clipped on about three-quarters of the way up the neck and, around the sound hole, a thin rosette, inlaid with abalone, that matched the fretboard to a T. It was a stunning piece of equipment. What a shame the boy had ruined it, Guillard thought, by placing all of those stickers over the front. When he finally responded, he barely acknowledged him, so intent as he was on his work, the strings vibrating in octaves and light harmonics and pentatonic scales, thirds and fourths. I'll keep that in mind, he said. What've you been talking about so far?

The story of Chang'e. Did you know that today is the Mid-Autumn Festival?

Of course. Didn't you?

No.

The boy laughed. Really?

You think I spend my time keeping track of Chinese holidays?

No, but people have been talking about it for weeks. I've been getting moon cakes all day. Haven't you?

Guillard ignored him and took a sheet from one of the kids and sat there studying the lyrics, trying to read what he could.

He had heard of neither the song nor the artist before. A holler went up from the kids as Daniel rose and strummed out a chord, telling them that he would sing the lyrics through one time so they could listen, a harmonica draped around his neck. The stand had been fashioned out of wire. When he started singing, the courtyard fell silent, the students under the oak tree holding their brooms, the girls in the audience regarding him softly, for he sang the lyrics with great soul. He was more than able on the harmonica, bending and sliding over the guitar, and the music carried far, drifting over the fields, the notes like a vesper—rolling, then still. The song spoke about love, and it went on forever—Guillard listening quietly from where he sat—and once Daniel had finished, he sang it again, this time enunciating each word. When Guillard looked up, there were at least twice as many students as before, and above the mountains, the moon had risen—what a fat and ugly bitch. He did not sing, for he had no rhythm, and after a while he wandered off, the only sound that of the students beneath the pavilion—Bella, as always, the loudest among the group.

五

On the weekends, Daniel would go riding, up through the hill-sides surrounding town, down through the paddies and quarries and aquaculture ponds that dotted the land. The roads were narrow but often untraveled, and the hamlets lay sleepy in the afternoons, no signs of occupancy but for the litter—occasionally, a dog. He followed the pavement for miles on end. The locals who saw him always seemed unsettled, for he came without warning, then he was gone—the young, tattooed foreigner with ears like the Buddha, hair the color of fire.

He had an excellent sense of direction, and he liked to return to the places he had been: a pine nursery, a swimming hole, an enormous precalcinator no longer in use. He welcomed forks, riding as far as his bike would go, feeling a certain freedom as he blazed his way farther into territories unknown. By that point, Daniel knew the country well, but there was always someplace new for him to explore, something new for him to learn. Just how this knowledge might serve him, he had no idea, but he did not care. For once, his life was exciting to him, in a way it had never been back home.

Three years out of college, and still the future was a blur. Who he was remained uncertain, although it was clearer than before. Ningyuan was not a permanent solution, he knew, but for the time being, it would serve. Somewhere out there, the next step awaited. He was not going to rush it. Much like that country, Daniel had retreated from the outside world, biding his time while developing his talents, and in many ways, he preferred to be alone. He was grateful for all of the opportunities he had been given, but somehow, they had never felt like enough. He was not ready to admit that he was average—whatever that meant. He had worked in an office and at a bar, and although teaching sometimes felt the same, it gave him the chance to pursue his interests and, while he did, travel, explore. He liked it better than he had imagined, but still it did not feel like what he was supposed to do, either. In any case, he had no regrets. Everything he had done had brought him to that point, and for the first time in about as long as he could remember, things were looking up.

The foothills were terraced about the road, like breakers washing onto shore, and wormwood grew in tangled clumps on what little could be seen of the shoulder. Daniel had been raised outside of the city, and from time to time he noticed the similarities, but this cheered him, for, growing up, he had never once taken issue with the land. The larger hills reared in the distance, jutting steeply from the floor, while behind them mountains loomed like sentinels, paling from green to blue to white. He motored past houses of fired mud as well as fisherfolk wading along the shores, blankets of rice spread out in the road awaiting the wheels of oncoming cars. He honked at those he passed but did not stop and try to talk, for their accents were thick to the point of unintelligibility, and his rides were themselves a form of escape.

He felt no animosity toward his students, but there were a few boundaries that had to be set. He had zero responsibilities on the weekends, and he hoped to keep it that way. They came to his door every Sunday, usually in groups of two or three, and since he was too polite to refuse them, Daniel often lost his afternoons. They would cook him lunch or take him hiking or sing him songs in the tents in the square, and if it was not them, it was the carpenter, trying to get him to practice English with his son. By that point, the two of them were like family, but, like family, there were times when he was not in the mood. By far, the worst was Connie. Whenever he came by, Daniel ended up drunk.

The other foreigners kept to themselves. He had not seen much of the Canadians, but he could hear them every so often, fighting or washing the dishes, never making love. They taught in a different building than he and Guillard did—an extension to the middle school abutting the road—which you had to walk through in order to exit the campus whenever the main gate was closed. The junior classes were even more crowded than his were, with upward of eighty students per room, and during the breaks between classes, children would loiter out on the railing like inmates, throwing paper into the yard. Daniel had taught six classes there the year before as a favor to the administration, but he had no desire to go back. They had paid him handsomely for it—eighty-five RMB an hour—but money was not his ambition, and besides, he valued his free time more. The Canadians were saving up for a trip to Cambodia, however, and they had leapt at the opportunity. As for Guillard, Daniel only saw him when the man needed help, and lately that was a lot.

Initially, he had wanted to switch classrooms. Because of his leg, he had trouble getting up the stairs, and Daniel had agreed that he should have the bottom two floors. James Li, however, was not so understanding. Their students had all of their classes in the same rooms throughout the year, and, therefore, moving would require great effort, since they kept all of their books and supplies inside of their desks. At approximately seventy students per room, what the foreigners were proposing was the relocation of more than two thousand kids. It was impossible, their liaison had told them. There was nothing that he could do. Thomas had lectured him on accessibility, citing the way things were usually done back home, and at one point, he had even threatened to default on his contract if his demands were not met. He had a way of talking down to others—especially the Chinese—and soon Daniel had heard enough. In the end, James Li had submitted, and the students had moved on a Sunday when, otherwise, they would have been out.

Since then, he had been asking for smaller things, but he had been asking more frequently, and with less courtesy. After he had moved in, Daniel had lent him the ladder he had built to change the bulbs in his room, but instead of thanking him, the man had just complained about the construction, probing mistrustfully at the joints. Once autumn arrived, he had enlisted Christopher and Daniel to help him move his television into his room, where there was a heater over the lintel and bottles of beer on the floor. He lived like a rodent, burrowing in trash, and there was a staleness to his apartment, as if he never went out.

Also, from what Bella had been telling him, it sounded like the man was stealing his lessons. Daniel had noticed him during their weekly meetings, squinting slantwise at his sheets, but he had chalked it up to curiosity. The job was easy—why plagiarize? Especially after his year at Yali. Famous inventions, the environment, planning a party, going out to eat. The choices were endless. James Li asked them to turn in their lessons, but he probably never checked. Hypothetical questions always worked: What would you say if you had ten seconds and the entire world was listening? If you suddenly came into a million dollars, what would you fear? The preparation was not difficult, provided you spoke English. So long as you got the kids talking, it did not matter what you taught.

He had thought about saying something at first, but this would have accomplished nothing. Daniel did not take himself so seriously, and if anyone appreciated the laxity of their situation, it was he. Thomas was a nuisance—both as a neighbor and a colleague—but he was also one of the reasons Daniel found China so strange. The place was like a playground for foreigners. For the most part, you were respected, and it was never hard to find work, and there were countless oddballs around every corner, exploiting their status for all it was worth. Thomas was not even one of the more outrageous characters he had met. The cities were full of them: blubbery old white men with no money but all of the confidence in the world.

That being said, he had thought himself safe in Ningyuan. One of the reasons he had requested a placement in the countryside was to get away from the people he knew, and, the previous year, there had only been one other foreigner, a man from Cameroon. They had been friendly but distant—which Daniel felt guilty about, now that the man was gone—since they had lived on opposite ends of the campus, taught different grade levels, and eaten on their own. Somewhat like the Canadians. Daniel did not have any problems with the new volunteers—especially since, as a couple, they kept to themselves—but the old man was another matter. During the three months he had been there, he had proven to be arrogant, lewd, and racist. He was giving the rest of them a bad name.

Daniel shifted gears and followed the course of the river beneath the gaze of the westering sun, admiring the haycocks out in the fields, the endless broken hills. The river was not wide, but the riverbed so, and a feeling of calmness came over his senses as he took it all in. He inhaled and caught a whiff of a duck farm upriver—an odor of shit and water and feathers—but aside from that, the air was clean. It made him ecstatic, without even drinking. He throttled past a couple of houses, where middle-aged men lay sleeping in rattan recliners in front of their doors, while, overhead, bowl-shaped antennae pointed skyward, set on a collection of rickety cairns. Somewhere behind the buildings, he could hear a chorus of elders singing a song from the revolution, extolling the CCP. By the time he was out of earshot, the landscape had turned to nothing but trees. Through the leaves, he could see the river. Boulders squatted in the shoals.

By and by, the road straightened, and in the distance, he made out a student. The jacket was unmistakable: white and orange and blue. Opening her up, Daniel leaned over the handlebars, feeling the muscles grow tight in his neck. He cut the distance in under a minute, and at the sound of his approach, the girl turned and started waving, trying to get him to stop. She was alone at the top of an embankment, looking up and down the road, and it was not until Daniel had pulled up onto the gravel next to her that he recognized who she was.

She was batting at a swarm of midges, and at first Daniel was unsure of whether he had interpreted her hand motions correctly. Behind her, he could hear the sound of the river drooling over the weir as well as the shouting of boys at play in the water, splashing and breaching the surface for air. The ravine was called Wuligou, owing to the distance it lay from town, and it ran through the fold of a shadowed vale, like some kind of kingdom unto itself.

Bella, he said. What are you doing out here on your own?

She looked at him, sulking. I invited you, remember? Today is the last day before examinations. I left a note on your door.

It took Daniel a moment before he remembered. Something about taking him on a hike, showing him the graves of her ancestors. He had read the note one evening after his classes but been so tired that he had forgot, and in all likelihood it was still sitting in the alcove next to the door, gathering dust. Daniel felt bad, but only a little. Shouldn't you be studying? he asked.

She did not answer, and in the silence, he suddenly got the feeling that there was something else wrong. Her eyes were red. Had she been crying? At her feet, he noticed a small plastic bag. Switching off the engine, he dismounted, crossing the road.

Hey, he said gently. Briefly, their eyes met. Is everything all right?

It doesn't help, she said. Always studying so much. I like to have a rest before my exams. Isn't that what Americans do? Besides, when I'm with you, I'm always practicing my English. She was speaking faster now, almost rambling. There was something crazed about her voice. I know you're busy—it's just that, for once, I was hoping to have some fun.

Again with the self-pity. Daniel reached out and touched her arm. Sorry, he said. I am. Who are you here with, your friends?

Bella looked down and kicked at the dirt next to the road, so fertile it was red. No, she said. Mr. Thomas. He's down there. She did not sound that excited, and Daniel could not blame her.

He drew himself up to the edge. Below them on the weir, several boys stood half-naked, water streaming over their ankles like ducks. Slightly upriver, a man with hair that was so matted it looked like the tail of a beaver could be seen scrubbing himself onshore, releasing soapsuds into the current, his clothing draped off the end of a branch. His groin was hairy in contrast to the rest of his body, and there seemed to be no sense of shame to his state of undress. Across the channel, a younger man with a bamboo pole fitted with an electrode was patrolling the shoreline, hunting for fish, but he was not the one Daniel was looking for either, and at this point he almost gave up. The boys on the weir noticed him and started waving, pointing emphatically toward shore, and as he followed their arms, he spotted a disembodied arc of urine, sprouting from behind a bush.

He frowned and turned back to Bella. She was staring up the road, as if expecting someone else.

How are classes going? he asked.

Classes?

With Mr. Thomas.

Oh, just so-so. He is humorous, but we aren't learning very much.

Here, Daniel had to contain himself. What did he teach you last week?

I don't know, actually. I was sick.

Really?

Yes. You didn't notice?

No, sorry.

But I wasn't at English Corner both days!

She was right. He remembered making note of her absence at the time. For once, he had been able to engage the other students and hold a general, group-wide discussion. It had been one of their most productive sessions to date. He turned and gazed across the river. Shadows creeping up the hills. How are you feeling now?

Better.

That's good. Not the best week to be feeling under the weather.

He had introduced this idiom to her before, and he was always trying to reinforce their lessons outside of class. Given the way Bella smiled at him, he could tell she knew what he was doing.

Can I ask you something? she said. About teaching.

Of course. Go ahead.

I was just wondering. What kind of training do you need? After graduating from university, I want to go abroad, too. I think life in the West must be very interesting, but I will need a job.

Well, most people have master's degrees nowadays.

Like you?

No. I studied philosophy in college. Imogen, Christopher, and I all went through a month of orientation, though. We have to send in reports to our organization at the end of every month. We should receive our TEFL certification soon.

But you don't have it now?

No, not at the moment.

How about Mr. Thomas?

Daniel shrugged. I'm not sure. He's not a part of our program, but he did teach at Yali last year. They wouldn't have hired him unless he had some kind of credential. To be honest, Daniel still could not believe the man had taught in Changsha. He was perhaps the most unprofessional-looking person he had ever met. That was China for you, though. Daniel had already begun to regret his decision to help him at the start of the year. Where do you want to teach? he asked.

Florence. Maybe Paris. I want to start a company for teaching Chinese somewhere in Europe.

You don't speak Italian or French, though.

So? Many foreigners in China don't know any Chinese.

Touché.

Pardon?

Nothing. It just means good point in French.

Bella nodded, quietly repeating the word to herself under her breath.

Why don't you just stay here and teach English? I'm sure you'd make a killing in one of the cities.

I've thought about that. It's just that—well, I don't know . . .

What?

Nothing. It's silly.

Come on, tell me. I'm your teacher.

She hesitated. All right. I don't know. It's hard to explain. It just feels like the older I get, the more distant I am becoming with my friends. We used to be close, but now it's like we have nothing in common.

I wouldn't worry about that. It's pretty normal. You're never gonna have as many friends as you do right now. Once you graduate, your social circle contracts, until one day you're married. Then you die.

Bella raised one eyebrow. She did not seem to get that it was a joke.

Still, she said. It's almost like we share completely different values. I am special. I know this. Sometimes I can barely stand to live in China. I imagine a life in which I have been born in Europe. That would be best . . .

Why not America?

Bella laughed. America is too dangerous. Everyone has guns! Where did you hear that?

You see it in all of the movies.

Now it was Daniel's turn to laugh. You can't believe what you see in Hollywood. I don't know a single person back home who owns a gun.

Bella considered this. Just as she was about to answer, a slew of curses came from the bush. Hacking his way up through the weeds, Guillard emerged at the base of the hill with one hand on his fly, which was giving him fits. He looked up and nodded at Daniel. If he was surprised at all to see him, he did not show it. It took him a minute to get up the embankment, and as he scrabbled over the rocks, Daniel and Bella stood there, watching him come on, like two considerate fools awkwardly holding a door.

When he reached the top, he bent over, wheezing, and lit a cigarette. Behind him, the boys on the weir were pointing in laughter and shouting Big Uncle Monkey at him in Chinese. One of them stooped down, using his knuckles for support, then began to lope across the obstruction until he slipped on some moss. He broke the water with a splash. A howl of laughter went up from his peers, but Guillard paid them no mind. It was equally likely he could not understand them—either that or his hearing was bad. He shot a look at Daniel's motorcycle, then spat in the dirt.

Can you believe this? he asked. Unbelievable.

Daniel could not tell what had upset him, but he was quick to agree. Sure is. In his voice, there was not the slightest hint of irony. Guillard peered at him through his owlish rims and a cloud of smoke. He did not offer Daniel a cigarette. His hands were dirty from the climb.

He was wearing the same clothes he had had on the first day the two of them had met—Velcro sandals, navy shorts, that god-awful, near-Hawaiian shirt—and, given the condition they were in, it did not seem as though he had washed them since. The inside of the collar was orange with sweat, and there were multiple soy stains down the front, and about his fly, there were a few blotches from where he had pissed himself while urinating in the bushes. The only new article in his wardrobe was a cheap yellow-and-green shirt, depicting the various positions of the kama sutra, enacted by a dragon and a phoenix to represent the sexes. Daniel had seen such shirts before, in one of China's more commercialized tourist traps, and at the time, he had asked himself who would ever want to buy such a thing, tacky as it was. Well, he thought, he finally had his answer.

Can that bucket-o'-bolts ride three? Guillard asked. He was pointing at the bike. It was covered in pollen and dust, and on the tank, Daniel had inscribed a large eye. The three of them turned to consider it, as if assessing the allowance for themselves.

It's fit four, once. Why? You need a ride?

Oh, sure. That would be great! He spoke sarcastically, his tone seeming to imply some kind of accusation, directed at Bella. We've been out here all day. I've got to get back to campus to meet with a student, if you know what I mean.

Daniel eyed him. Given the man's attitude toward teaching, this seemed unlikely. Probably just an excuse. Then he noticed Guillard's hand. It was clutched firmly over his stomach, implying, discreetly, that he had to shit. Daniel looked at Bella, who was not participating in the conversation, then turned away and squinted up the road. There was nothing there. How did you get out here? he asked.

Bella answered. By taxi. Our driver promised to come back at noon, but I think he forgot.

You think? Guillard snorted. It's already half past two.

Why didn't you just walk?

Guillard rolled his eyes at the suggestion. What are we, ten miles outside of town?

Five kilometers, actually.

Guillard nodded sarcastically, as though he believed Daniel to be making light of the situation. You going to help us or not?

Of course. No problem. I can take you back.

Really? Bella said. Her voice echoed through the hills. Guillard's eyes narrowed almost imperceptibly, as though he were deathly hungover. Thank you, Teacher Daniel!

Yeah, thanks.

It's not a big deal. Really.

Oh, by the way, Bella said, remembering the bag at her feet. This is for you.

What is it? Opening the bag, he discovered a clump of fried rice balls, glisteningly sweet.

Tangyou baba. My grandmother made them this morning.

Guillard took one last pull from his cigarette, then stomped it out in the dirt. That stuff'll rot your teeth out, he said. Take it from me.

Daniel ignored him and turned to Bella. *San ke you wei ni ma chi.*

For the first time that afternoon, she smiled. Wow! You are like a native Chinese!

They collected their belongings and mounted up, trying to settle on a workable arrangement on his bike, and as they did, an open tuk-tuk went by, the driver eyeing them queerly from where he sat. Guillard had trouble getting himself onto the bike, and Daniel had to lower the frame to the ground—like a camel or an elephant, kneeling on its forelegs to take on a rider. Bella sat on the

crash rack, her jacket folded beneath her rump, and as they nes-
tled into each other, she started humming, right into Guillard's ear.
The entrance to the swimming hole lay on an incline, and Daniel
had to build up speed slowly, coaxing the gears against the weight
of their bodies, rocking his shoulders for added push. Once they
crested the ridge, it was all sunlight—the floodplains stretched out
across the valley below them—and, on the way down, they passed
through a pocket of cold air. Then they were off.

Guillard was bony and, as a result, uncomfortable at Daniel's
back, and he was an obsessive backseat driver, even though the
road was fairly straight. Still, Daniel preferred him there to Bella,
who, the last time they had ridden, had wrapped her arms around
his chest tightly, begging him to go fast. He could not hear what
she was saying now, but her mood seemed to have improved, for,
by the time they climbed the last rise into town, her humming had
turned into song. They stalled out on the way down, and behind
him Daniel heard a snort of derision come from Guillard, but by
letting out the clutch, he was able to push start the engine, and that
shut the man up. The farmers were back from their lunches in the
fields, riding outlandish jerry-rigged machines. Beside the road,
countless haycocks had been stacked like medieval tanks, drying
in the sun.

He dropped Bella and Guillard off at the gate, then went to
park at the carpenter's house. Three locals were coming home from
a banquet, but when they saw him, they did not stop. They looked
to be over forty, and the two on the outside were wearing glasses,
and the one in the middle was slumped between their shoulders,
like some injured player being carted off the pitch. By the color of
their faces, the other two were not doing well, either. Overhead,
a crescent moon had risen above the mountains, and between its
horns, Jupiter and Venus were visible, forming, all together, a lecherous grin. The carpenter was not home, so Daniel left his bike on
the curb, then made his way back to his apartment, completely

lost as to what he might do. It was Sunday, and he was restless, and what else was there to do other than sleep or drink or masturbate? Sometimes, he wished he knew.

六

Come nightfall in the country, there was little fun to be had. The streets were lined with tea shops and vendors, but there were no taverns, no bars. Guillard would set off walking from campus, a fresh pack of Shuangxi in one hand, and by the time he pulled up in front of the Confucian temple, half of them would be gone. The square was home to various attractions—a carousel, KTV tents, games of skill, games of chance—and as he sat there slurping his noodles, he would listen to the Chinese sing, and he would laugh.

After dinner, he would go to the market, semitumescent in the road, the local women eyeing him shyly, their bodies so perfect, their faces jake. Guillard had lowered his standards since coming to Ningyuan, as all of the younger, more beautiful girls had left for the cities along the coast. The ones who remained were either overly traditional or too stuck up to approach. Guillard was focused on finding an older woman, but when on occasion he tried to hit on them, they would either feign confusion or laugh at what he said or even, in some cases, run off. He did not take this for discouragement—it was a matter of numbers, and they were scared—and a man had to try if he wanted to get laid, and, anyway, what else was there to do?

On a night in December, as he was passing Every Day, an Internet bar favored among the youths, he found a construction worker dead on the street, a fold of cardboard over his face. A crowd had formed in front of the scaffolding, blankly regarding the scene, but no one had called to alert the authorities—at least, that was how it seemed. He hung back at the edge of their number, quietly listening to the man's wife, who knelt by the curb, keening wildly, beating her breasts with the flats of her wrists. The dead man's clothes were plain, like those of a farmer, and from the look of his blood, he had been dead for some time. Behind them, a newly finished elevator shuttled passengers up and down the building, like a glass-encased remora, lighting the square.

He had yet to eat, but he was thirsty, and that took priority for the moment. He crossed the square and bought a beer, drinking the contents in one pull. A table applauded and bought him another and had him repeat this for their friends, one man challenging him to a race, for, as it seemed, he had a reputation to uphold. Pouring half of the beer down his shirt, the drunk smiled, then turned and said something to his friends—the rest of the Chinese already standing, roaring in ovation, no sense of honor among these men. They exchanged cigarettes, invited him to dinner, then asked him why he was there, where he was from, and although Guillard had been cheated, he sat down and obliged them, taking what he wanted of their liquor, their food.

By the time he left, the world was warmer, and it felt like a place he could actually use—the bulbs on the food carts brighter, more beautiful, the people somehow closer to him than before. Two boys on a bicycle came through the crowd, wobbling slightly, ringing a bell, and Guillard fell in behind them, for despite winter's arrival, the roads were just as full. A couple stopped him and handed him their child and, without warning, photographed him using their phone—the image a queer one, Guillard standing there stupefied, the child bubbling out of its nose. In one of the drink stores he went into, there were hundreds of Post-it notes lining the walls, and after browsing them, Guillard noticed two that caught his attention:

NINGYUAN SAVED MY LIFE!

TEACHER DANIEL SAVED MY LIFE!

He purchased a bottle of wine to keep things going—a Chinese red that was far too astringent—but, mixed with soda, it was not half bad. He drank it slowly, wandering the town.

As he started back in the direction of Yi Zhong, he made out someone with long red hair. He stood by the food carts ordering a meal, surrounded by others mostly his age. Whether he was out riding or up on the roof, Daniel never seemed to be home, and other than the two days they spent teaching English Corner together, they rarely socialized. Guillard did not care. Still, he had taken to wondering where the boy went, for there was something strange in the way he would disappear. It was as if Guillard and the others did not even deserve an explanation—as if he had more important things to do—and standing there, bottle in hand, Guillard felt somehow satisfied to know that what he did was actually nothing—nothing at all.

He followed the group as they entered the square, Daniel in the middle, leading the way, the Chinese hovering around him and laughing at his jokes, hanging off every word he said. He had on a striped beanie that was also red, and his hair was like that of a girl, and he seemed to have lost a few pounds since the last time they had seen each other. Guillard trailed at a distance, nursing his wine. A couple of men shouted at the boy, but when Guillard walked by, they hardly noticed him, huddling closer to confer in measured whispers as to what they had just seen. In the boy's wake, Guillard knew that he was just an afterthought, and although he enjoyed the anonymity, a pang of resentment came, too. There was a glassblower next to the fountain, crafting trinkets on demand, and this had attracted a crowd of the locals, the flame of the torch caught in their eyes.

Daniel and his friends stopped to admire the process. The man had just started a piece from scratch. Using his blowpipe, he reached into the furnace, then gathered a blob of the vitreous goo. He spooled the stuff slowly, like honey from a jar. On his cart were various animals he had created that night, and in the glow of the molten glass, they seemed an unsightly menagerie. Monkeys and lions and dogs, their bodies all perfectly segmented, like ants. Once the glass had been rolled and the exterior cooled, he went to work, blowing down the tube, rotating it delicately on the rail, the shapes now forming out of nothing but his will—that and hot air. When he was finished, he returned it to the fire, then wiped his hands as he set it to anneal. Glancing up, he noticed Daniel, and at the sight of him, he smiled. He beckoned the boy and his friends closer, fishing through his wares, and offered him a bear.

The crowd dispersed, and as it did, Guillard stepped forward, calling his name. Given the noise in the square, it was difficult to hear, and neither Daniel nor his friends turned around. They started walking, chewing their food, spitting their bones in the street, and, lugging his foot, Guillard had to hurry, brushing past the shoulders of others to keep up. Unlike Changsha, there were no tall buildings in Ningyuan, and above the square, it was only darkness, that and the light of the myriad stars. To the south, he marked Orion, racked on the edge of a distant bluff, receding gradually over the horizon, like a man out of reach, drowning in space.

By the time he caught up to Daniel and the others, they were standing in front of a stage. On it, a young woman was hosting a show that had to do with matching couples from the audience. She was not very pretty, but she was trying to be, her face powdered so heavily in makeup that it looked like clay beneath the lights. Standing behind Daniel, Guillard cleared his throat. Then he clapped the boy on the shoulder.

You looking for a girlfriend? he asked.

When the boy turned around to face him, Guillard was surprised to find that it was a girl. She smiled at him at first, still thinking him a friend, but when it became clear who it was that had touched her, she grew scared. Without thinking, she slapped him—hard. The sound was muffled by the crowd. She had the same color hair as Daniel, even though, up close, it was much less bright, and after a moment, Guillard quit cursing. He held up his hands, studying her face.

She was an absolute beauty. He wanted to break her in half. As Guillard stood there, imitating surrender, the boys around her eyed him, posturing where they stood. One of them Guillard thought he recognized from class. The crowd around them started cheering at the sudden sound of an electric bass, while up on stage, two contestants stood blushing, the hostess urging them to kiss. Guillard could feel the boys getting hotter. He smiled nervously, then let down his arms. The girl was shouting something at him in Chinese, but it was too fast for him to follow. He pointed at her hair, trying to explain.

Wo juede ni shi biede ren le.

One of the boys laughed. The girl gave him an odd look, but it seemed as if she understood. Her features were plainspoken, like that of a doll—unblemished yet ripe—and the tuque she had on made her look even cuter, the tassels like pigtails, framing her face.

Wo jiao Thomas. *Ni ne?*

She would not tell him. All she did was look at the others, then wrinkle her nose, stare at the ground. Finally, she mumbled hello.

Ni WOW! he responded, smiling as he hitched up his brow. Behind her, the two contestants had finally caved. The man sidled up next to the woman, then pecked her on the cheek. By the way the crowd reacted, you would have thought they were going at it.

Guillard refocused his attention. He asked the girl if she had a boyfriend, pointing toward the stage.

With one last look, she nodded, a certain vacancy to her eyes. She turned toward the platform and waded through the crowd and disappeared with the boys at her back. Guillard glowered, but he did not linger there long. With the music as loud as it was and the effect of the alcohol starting to wane, he felt irritable and partnerless. He took another swig. The hostess was soliciting new volunteers from the crowd, and he watched as they hoisted the girl onstage. Not one to acknowledge his failures, he lit a fresh cigarette. Then he walked away.

The wife of the deceased was still on the sidewalk, and to avoid her, he cut down an alley, where household gods and red paper lanterns hung from the doorways, the eaves overhead. Several doors were open, and as he passed, he saw his shadow on the walls, like that of a puppet—all loose strings and wood—being handled from above. Ahead in the darkness, a cur growled. Guillard proceeded cautiously, stepping over piles of brick, hods of coal, yet, still, when he saw the dog, he was almost on top of it. Fortunately, the animal was preoccupied with something else. It stood with its head down, eyeing the mouth of the alley, where, across the street, a mound of offal had been dumped and left to rot until morning. It was an old, slat-ribbed mongrel, with piebald markings on its coat. Skirting the alley's wall, Guillard peered into the trash. A younger, healthier dog lay sprawled atop the mound. When it noticed him, it bared its teeth, then went back to work on a bone.

During the day, the street was a market, and to one side, it bordered the People's Hospital, a low, jaundice-colored building that spanned a length of a thousand feet. With dawn, butchers and greengrocers would appear, forming a gauntlet of wains and stalls, the older, poorer folk slouched beneath the windows, from which came the sounds of groans and coughs. There were no streetlights. Guillard hobbled past the building and emerged up the road from

Yi Zhong, down to the dregs of his hundred-kuai bottle, his lips stained purple, his eyes a fright. The road was dark, except for one building, a converted row house along the bank—a sort of pool hall, from the looks of it. A crowd had gathered in the street.

He wandered past to have a look and heard the word *laowai* among the talk, but it had not been made in reference to him, for he was behind whomever had said it. He could not see into the hall, but he heard the clacking and thud of balls as well as the lighter sound of table tennis rackets, driving points home. He muscled through the crowd. Toward the front, there were several students dressed in uniforms, rooting Daniel on. At one of the pool tables, he saw the boy, aligning his shot like a pro.

The students recognized Guillard, but none of them were in his classes. He said hello, then crossed the room, coming up behind the boy as he rose. His shot had stalled by half a rotation. Chuckling, Guillard set down his bottle, then studied the shape of the balls. He was already on to another cigarette. He exhaled through his nose.

You gotta hit it, ya?

Daniel eyed him and holstered his cue. He had on a cap similar to the one the girl had been wearing, though he did not pull it off so well.

Thomas.

You should've gone for the seven there. Would've left you in a better position.

Daniel did not answer. He looked at the wine on the table. D-Y-nasty, he said.

Huh?

Dynasty. He pointed at the label. Give me all of the baijiu in China—I try to avoid that stuff.

Guillard frowned. I didn't buy it for the taste.

The boy bent down and potted the five. Behind them, one of his students cheered. *Hao qiu.* Daniel stood up and circled the balls. What have you been up to? he asked.

Same-old. You?

Things've been crazy busy lately. Between classes, grading, and English Corner, I haven't had time for anything else.

What is there to grade? You heard James the other day—all he expects us to do is show up.

Daniel shrugged. He stood at one end of the table, chalking his cue. Assignments, quizzes, homework. I try to keep the kids accountable, best I can. Otherwise, it's too hard to get them involved.

You grade homework for all of your students?

Well, no. Not exactly. They're divided into groups. I keep them on a rotation.

Guillard stood there, shaking his head. I've been hearing a lot of you lately, up on the roof. What's that all about?

Just this project I've been working on. I got into carpentry last year. It's become something of a hobby.

What are you building?

The boy paused, as though debating whether or not to tell him. An aeolian harp, he finally said.

Eh?

It's a musical instrument played by the wind. I figure that after I'm gone, it'll still be here. Kind of like my own personal mark on Yi Zhong.

Guillard laughed and rolled his eyes, changing the subject. You see that poor old dead bastard in the street?

Gently, Daniel kissed the four off one of his opponent's balls, but again it came up short. Yeah, he said. Actually, I was there when it happened.

Jesus Christ. Really?

Without much thought, Daniel's opponent fired away. There was a brief silence as the balls went caroming off the rails. The man was a banger, plain and simple, and, like Daniel, he could not make consecutive shots. Still, he appeared confident. Like most of the other locals, he was wearing a glove. He reminded Guillard of Feng, the principal at Yi Zhong, for both men were built like pit bulls, and they wore the same clothes.

How come you didn't call someone? Guillard asked. The guy's still out there, you know, bleeding in the street.

It's complicated.

Complicated? More like barbaric. His wife is tearing her hair out, and no one even lifts a finger.

Daniel refocused and sunk the three. Only the eight ball remained. His wife is the one keeping him there, he said.

What?

The family wants compensation. Workers don't have a lot of rights out here. The only leverage they have is the corpse.

You gotta be kidding me.

Unfortunately not. They think that by leaving the body in front of the work site, it'll cause the owner to lose face. They'll build a coffin, but until they get their money, they aren't going anywhere.

Guillard snorted. Good luck with that.

You'd be surprised. With his bridge hand, he tucked a strand of hair behind one of his ears, then lowered his eyes to the table, surveying his approach. Last year, a baby died in the hospital across the street. Foot and mouth. I discovered the body one night, walking back to school. The family had dumped it right in the middle of the street, for everyone to see. I couldn't believe it. By morning, it was gone. From what I heard, the hospital paid, although I don't know how much. Coming up out of his squat, he set himself, then called the corner pocket, and after perhaps the most prolonged series of practice strokes Guillard had ever seen, he put away the eight. From the doorway, more applause.

What the hell's wrong with these people?

Daniel was shaking his opponent's hand and conversing with him in Chinese, like a brother. I wouldn't be so quick to judge, he said. It's terrible, I agree, but living out here isn't easy.

You're telling me.

The boy looked at him. I mean for them.

Guillard finished the rest of his bottle and set it on a thin ledge of wood along the wall. Daniel's opponent had left, and the boy was returning the cue he had been using to the rack. It was not yet ten o'clock. Toward the front, most of the spectators had already left, but Daniel's students were still there, hoping for another game. There was smoke in the air. Somewhere, someone was burning trash.

You wanna play? Guillard asked.

Daniel paused. Sure, he finally said. He did not turn around. I'm gonna get a drink first, though. You want one?

Hao de.

Rack 'em.

He watched the boy go. There was an icebox next to the pool hall's great tambour door, and as Daniel approached, the proprietor rose, greeting him warmly. Like everyone else in town, he appeared to be a friend. Guillard shagged the balls from their pockets and looked under the table, but in the end came up empty. There was no triangle to be found. At the table next to them, a group of boys was playing cutthroat and Fight the Landlord, folding their hands down onto the rail whenever their turns came to shoot. He borrowed a rack from them, but they did not lend it to him freely. On one's shirt, the words SCHOOL SUCKS had been printed in English. He did not look much older than most of Guillard's students. Then again, with the Chinese, it was impossible to tell.

Daniel came back and handed him a beer. It was warm, and there was something sticky on the glass. As the boy broke, Guillard took a long draft, the balls exploding, then caroming off the bumpers, until at last they came to rest. They sat like show pieces atop their shadows on the smooth, faultless baize. Guillard set down his beer and picked up a cue. Then he went to work.

He made the first couple of balls with great facility, studying the table like a map, ignoring the encouragements of Daniel's students, shrewdly positioning his shots. He felt the boy's surprise, but a blustering amateur he was not, and when he kicked his next shot into the corner, it clattered between the jaws before dropping.

Hao qiu, Daniel said.

Guillard grunted in response.

The boy lit a cigarette. How've your classes been going?

Guillard frowned. He had missed the next shot. Christ, he said. Don't ask me that. All I wanna do is relax. He pointed at the table. C'mon, your shot.

That bad?

These kids don't have any motivation. Can you really blame them, though? Most are gonna wind up as farmers, tradesmen, cooks. I doubt half of them ever make it out of Ningyuan. What good is English going to do them?

Daniel was in midstroke, but when he heard this, he stopped. I'd beg to differ, he said. He resumed his stance, then made his shot. An attitude like that only perpetuates the system. Just because our students are up against increased odds doesn't mean you should deny them resources. Do you have any idea how crazy that sounds? Self-righteously, he pushed past Guillard, chalking his cue. Besides, who are you to decide their fate?

Guillard bristled at Daniel's tone. If there was one thing he could not stand, it was idealism.

Let me ask you a question, he said. Do you think we're even making a difference here?

Daniel considered the lay of the balls, and during the time it took him to respond, Guillard finished the rest of his beer. I don't know, he said. That's not what I try to focus on. I just try to do my best every day. If you're asking me, though, then yes: I do.

There was a moment during which they just stood there, eyeing each other. Then Guillard began to laugh. Hallelujah! he shouted. An awkward silence filled the room. The other patrons turned to look at him as Daniel glowered, flushing slightly, but this did not discourage him. All rise and hail the *laowai* who has come to save your souls!

Slowly, the conversations returned. The boy across from them with an aversion to school marked Guillard with his cue and called him a *shenjingbing*, which, after so many years in China, he had been called more than once before. Daniel bent down and aimed at the twelve, but when he fired, it did not go in. He said nothing by way of rejoinder, a sullen expression lining his face.

Oh, come on. I'm kidding, ya?

I just don't think it's funny, is all. He lifted his bottle and drank. Whereas Guillard had already finished, he was only about halfway through. Their eyes met across the table. How about Bella? Daniel asked.

What about her?

Don't you think she benefits from us being here?

Guillard stopped and considered this. Behind him, the boys at the next table were laughing and calling him names. He turned to stare them down, but this only seemed to encourage them.

A girl like Bella would be able to find ways to practice her English whether or not we were here. Yi Zhong doesn't give a damn about our classes. And you can bet your ass our students don't, either.

That's not the point. Who's the teacher here anyway, them or you? James and the others care about our classes—otherwise why would they offer to pay us extra to teach on the weekends? They need us, and they're happy with how we've been doing. That much, I think, is clear.

Guillard snorted. That's not the impression I get. Anyway, I'm not here looking for approval. He leaned down the best his body would allow and reviewed the options in front of him. Plus, he said, staring across the table, unlike some people, I don't need the cash.

They stopped talking and focused all of their attention on the game, and, in time, the increasingly palpable air of competition around them drew another crowd. The boys at the next table seemed to be actively rooting against Guillard. At one point, two of them used their sticks to cut his knees out from under him, but Daniel turned and scolded them in Mandarin, which caused them to stop. Guillard took the ball in hand, mentally tallying the score, then lit a cigarette and set it down on the edge of the rail. He still had four balls left, including the eight, but he could see the run he was about to go on before him, like a skein of injured ducks. He set the cue ball down and aligned his shot, then, very lightly, dropped the six.

The rest of his balls were well positioned, but by that point it did not matter. He had the cue ball on a string. He cinched one ball after the next, taking pulls of tobacco in between, the Chinese watching him and muttering in approval, clearly impressed by his skill. Guillard ignored them, moving from shot to shot as if he had been there before. By the time he made his last ball, they were firmly on his side, but he had positioned himself poorly to put away the eight. Daniel only had one ball remaining. It was behind the head string, however—stuck against a wall—and after a moment's thought, Guillard decided it best to scratch.

Really? Daniel whined.

You gotta know how to play the game.

The boy palmed the ball and studied the angle. From the way it looked, it would have to be one hell of a shot. He selected a location in the middle of the table that was more or less on line with the ball, then backed away and rolled up his sleeves. Then he picked it up again. Offsetting it slightly this time, he leaned down and dragged his eyes over the table. The Chinese whispered over his tattoos, like a nervous band of aunts. He did not seem to hear them. Finally, he struck the ball, holding his posture as it rolled, and when he hit it, the girls near the entrance came over, clapping and fretting and shouting *jiayou!* At first, it seemed like it might have a chance, but on the way back, it tailed off, and Daniel was left dancing up alongside the rail, like a motley-clad fool. A communal groan swept the room.

The boy had left him a perfect shot. *Xiexie guanglin,* Guillard said, pocketing the eight. Thank you, come again.

About half of the spectators cheered. The other half did not. Guillard bowed and made his way over to the wall rack, storing his cue among the rest. Behind him, he could hear the boys at the next table mocking him, shouting in English and dragging their feet. Daniel came over, unenthusiastically, and congratulated him.

By now, Guillard was drunk, but he was only getting started. That mean the next round is on you, too? he asked. To taunt the boy, he removed the stick from its sheath and tucked it between his legs, wagging it back and forth. You just let me know, *shuaige.* I'm ready to go again.

Before Daniel could answer, everything went black. Someone had crept up behind him and clapped their hands over his face, and, without thinking, Guillard wheeled on the assaulter, swinging as hard as he could. The cue connected with Bella's temple, quivering up and down its length, but despite the considerable force of impact, it did not break. The pool hall fell dead silent. Bella collapsed to the floor. Players at neighboring tables turned and set down their bottles, regarding Guillard darkly from where they stood. Daniel, who had already rushed over, was kneeling down next to Bella, checking her for injuries while he tried to calm the crowd. Eventually he looked up at Guillard.

What the hell's wrong with you? he said.

七

They were informed of their three-day weekend on Friday morning by Mr. Cai, who came to their apartments and beat on the
doorframes until the four of them were up. From his room at
the end of the hall, Daniel could hear Guillard in the stairwell—
complaining in English, cursing James Li—but by the time he
opened the door, his neighbor was already gone. Where he had
stood, a cigarette lay burning, like a desperate, glowing coal, while
next to it, a spot of saliva reflected the light from the clouds overhead. Daniel had forgotten to cover the hatch, and this had clearly
upset the man, for there was a message taped onto his ladder. All
it said was WHAT GIVES?

It had been raining since midnight, and Mr. Cai did not look
pleased. His hair was drenched, and due to the weather, his shoes
were ruined, spattered with mud. He took one look at Daniel,
water rolling down his face, then turned and flapped one hand at
the ladder, propped the other against the door. You cannot leave
this here, he said. Yes? It must be moved. Now!

They lived on the top floor of the building, and in two years,
Daniel had never seen anyone else come up aside from his students

and the administration, but he did not feel like fighting. He lifted one of the crosspieces onto his shoulder, then carried it into the parlor, where he leaned it against the wall. Mr. Cai followed him inside. He had the look of a bedraggled chicken, and he was dripping all over the floor.

You want a towel? Daniel asked.

No. It is not necessary. He removed his glasses, buffing them with his shirt. I only come to tell you there will be no classes on Monday.

When he heard this, all Daniel could do was shake his head. That Sunday was the twenty-fifth of December, and his friend, Neil, who lived in Changsha, had invited him to visit. Since late November, he and the Canadians had been trying to work on James Li, but there was no way to switch their classes, and in the end, their liaison would not allow them to leave. Due to the distance, traveling to the capital in two days was possible but by no means fun, and as a result, Daniel had turned down Neil's offer. Another Christmas in Ningyuan.

Why not? he asked. Somehow, he had a feeling religious observance had nothing to do with it.

Examinations. It is almost the end of the month.

A little advance notice would have been nice. Imogen and I have been asking for some time off now for weeks. It's Christmas, you know.

Mr. Cai scowled as he turned out the door. This is China. Not USA!

————

He woke up early the next morning and packed his toiletries in the dark, brushing his teeth in the cold of the bathroom, feeding the chickens, clearing the sink. The streets were empty save for a noodle cart, and but for a grayness above the hills, there was little to be seen as he trudged across town. He bought some baozi from a man with one good eye on Jiuyi Lu and responded to all of the vendor's questions regarding life in the West. The cost of goods. The balance of power. The habits of black people. The weather. The food. The vendor's eyelid was folded shut in the manner of a boxer who had just lost a fight, and this gave him a strange look of misgiving as he counted Daniel's change. He listened to what the boy said, nodding at times, and when Daniel left, he wished him safe travels, inviting him to visit once he was back.

The lot in front of the station was freezing and smelled like gasoline, and the bus was surrounded by those yet to board. He waited and ate beneath the overhang, shifting back and forth on his heels to stay warm. He had bought his ticket the night before, but there were still plenty of seats left, and as he chewed, his jaw clicked like a pair of loose stones.

Life had been dull since Thanksgiving, and Daniel was ready to see his friend. Although he and Neil had hardly spoken in over a year, he felt just as close to him as they had been during his first month in Hunan. That seemed like long ago, now. Classroom training, drinking in hotel rooms, counting down the weeks, then days, till Ningyuan. It had been a confusing, exciting time. The mood of the program was much like college, and as Daniel had been—and, in all honesty, still was—searching for something else, he had distanced himself from the others, exploring the city on his own. He was looking for an authentic view of China, but what exactly did that mean? Pondering this, he frowned. Sometimes, he felt like a fraud.

He had met Neil on Hualongchi, a cobblestone alley that was full of bars, and the Brit had been so drunk that he had thrown one arm over Daniel's shoulders, regaling him with song. He had not been with any others, but everyone else seemed to know him, and as they walked, the locals came over and sang with him, smiling, crowding about. From the moment they first met, it had been clear there was something about him—a certain mischievousness mixed with wits—and this was hard to not like. They had spent the rest of the night in a bar, smoking a hookah, shooting dice, and, on their way home, they had stopped by the river, feasting on *shaokao*, miserable, drunk.

God, Daniel thought. Would that this weekend be like that.

He boarded the bus and turned on some music. Toward the front, an old woman was running the count. When she was finished, she turned to the driver, then told him the number and got off. The driver frowned. Apparently, they were short. They sat in the lot with the engine off and waited in silence, trying to sleep, until, several minutes later, the driver grew restless and, standing up, proceeded to honk. Exactly what this was meant to accomplish Daniel had no idea, but somehow it worked, for, after a couple of tries, he paused, straining his ears at the sound of a response.

The cab sped into the station like a race car, swerving around potholes, kicking up dust, and when it was the Canadians who emerged from the back, Daniel could see that they were fighting. Christopher, heavy with sleep, got both of their bags from the trunk, then carried them on, apologizing to the driver, immediately passing out. From where he sat, Daniel watched Imogen— her eyes obscured behind huge sunglasses—pay the driver, then come down the aisle, settling in a few rows back. As far as he could tell, she had not seen him. Discarding his cigarette, the driver started the engine, then closed the door and looked toward the back, announcing to those who were listening that they were not going to stop. Daniel remained in his seat until they had made it to the freeway, then got up and went over to say hi, grasping the seat tops like a sailor, his long red hair cowled beneath a hood.

Imogen was reading when he approached. She did not look up. Daniel stood there for a moment, then leaned in, smiling over her shoulder.

Meinü, he said playfully. *Zai kan shenme ne?*

Defiantly, she glared up at him, but when she realized who it was, the expression softened. She closed her book and sighed in relief.

Daniel, she said. Sorry. I thought you were Chinese.

He smiled and seated himself across the aisle. They were somewhere outside of Yongzhou, but it had started raining again, and through the window, all you could see were the mountains, the lambent clouds veiling their slopes. Imogen turned and took off her glasses. Her eyes were swollen, most likely from lack of sleep. What did you ask? she said.

What are you reading. Leaning across the aisle, he pointed at her lap.

Oh. Just this book about India. I bought it before I knew I was coming to China. She lifted the cover for him to see. On it, an elephant stood with its trunk on its forehead, holding a giant pink lotus. Ahead of them, a tractor appeared, going back in the direction they had come. When the driver saw it, he honked, causing both of them to jump.

Looks like we got our vacation after all, Daniel said, smiling cautiously. You two cut it pretty close, though.

Imogen frowned at him, then looked out the window. It wasn't my fault, she said. We had to go back.

Wallet?

Passport. I must have told him about a thousand times.

Well. You made it. That's all that counts. Why do you need it? Are you two going to stay in a hotel?

She nodded. You?

I'm gonna crash with Neil. He lives downtown, right across from Walking Street. Pretty sweet location. Leaning back, Daniel let down his hood. His hair was greasy and tangled in knots. A nylon band to hold it in place. What are your plans for the weekend? he asked.

Imogen shrugged. Oh, the usual, I guess. Groceries, maybe a movie. Dinner with some friends. A group of volunteers from our year is throwing a party at Lushan tonight. That's close to Walking Street, isn't it? She caught his eye, and when she did, she smiled. You should come.

I don't know. I don't know any of the current volunteers. Plus, I bet Neil's already made plans.

So? Bring him. There's gonna be a ton of people there. A lot of cute girls . . .

Daniel blushed. We'll see.

OK, she said, laughing. I'm not gonna push. Seriously, though, I think you should come. I mean it! It would be nice to hang out—just the three of us—for once.

Can't argue with you there.

Imogen frowned and crossed her legs, then dog-eared the page she was on and set down the book. That's another reason we were late this morning. Thomas buttonholed me on the stairs. I'm pretty sure he was drunk. Eight o'clock in the morning, and he's already sauced . . .

Daniel sat there, shaking his head. What did he want?

He wanted me to go out and buy him cigarettes. Can you believe that? Seems like ever since he hit Bella, the entire town has turned against him. And rightfully so. He's so scared he won't even leave campus. He told me that the last time he did, someone spit on him. Anyway, the whole time, I'm just standing there, trying to escape, until finally Chris comes back up and—get this—tells him to FUCK OFF. I almost burst out laughing. You should have seen the look on his face.

Chris said that?

Right hand to God.

Jesus. Your boyfriend is my hero.

Imogen smiled. He's definitely not a morning person. I'll give you that.

Daniel gazed out the window. The bus was climbing in low gear up the side of a gorge, where stands of bamboo hung out over the pavement like enormous, hard-bodied ferns. Owing to the fog, it was hard to see into the distance, and for a moment he forgot where he was. Turning back to Imogen, he studied her face.

How did Thomas react?

He just stood there, staring at us. Then he went back inside. Chris says he's one of those people who doesn't get how he comes off—needs to be put in his place every now and again. Me? I'm not so understanding. To be honest, he creeps me out.

How's that?

I don't know. Something about his laugh. That and the fact that he always seems to be staring at—she stopped herself. Well, not at my eyes.

He's hard to get along with, Daniel conceded. That's for sure. Every time I try to reach out, he finds some way to make me regret it. Like when we were playing pool the other night. I believe him that it was an accident, but still, there's no excuse. I swear, I'm on the verge of giving up.

What happened, exactly?

We'd just finished a game, and Bella came up behind him. There'd been a group of boys next to us, giving him shit, and I guess he thought she was one of them.

Poor Bella.

Yeah. I think it goes without saying that he was drunk. Anyway, the crowd turned on him pretty fast. We had to fight our way out of the room, and a bunch of the Chinese followed us back to Yi Zhong. Fortunately, Yang was still up. He wouldn't let them past.

Who's Yang?

The guard at the gate.

Oh. Baldy or squints?

Daniel smiled. The bald one, he laughed.

It's scary. Chris and I were coming out of the supermarket yesterday, and a crowd gathered at the sight of us. I guess that doesn't sound too out of the ordinary, but a few of them were shouting. They seemed upset. At the time, we didn't know what was going on. It was only later, once we got back to our apartment, that we figured it out.

Yeah, I've been noticing that, too. The Chinese have a history with foreigners. It's complicated. They either hate us or love us. There's no middle ground.

Do you think we'll be safe here for the rest of the year?

Absolutely, Daniel said, shooting her a bemused look. Don't worry, I'm sure that all of this will have blown over by the time we get back.

Good. Sounds like this vacation came at just the right time, then. A couple of days without Thomas—what more could we ask?

Daniel smiled. The two of them spoke a while longer, discussing their classes and Christmases past, until Christopher woke up and came over, still groggy from sleep. If he was surprised at all to see Daniel, he did not show it. The skin above his eyelids was red and deeply furrowed from the way in which he had been sleeping, and one glance was all it took to see that he was ready to make up. Daniel took his cue and went back to his seat, leaning his head against the glass. The man beside him let him in, then removed his shoes and dozed back off, the cabin quiet now, aside from the engine, each traveler riding alone with his thoughts.

———

The rain had quit by the time they reached Changsha, but Neil, as usual, was not answering his phone. Daniel had called him the night before to let him know that he was coming, and Neil had told him to call once they were close—they would decide where to meet from there. Since Zhuzhou, Daniel had been dialing, but the line just kept ringing—a gaudy pop song in his ear—until, at last, it began to go straight to a recording saying the phone had been switched off. Most likely, Neil was in a meeting—since they had met, he had always had at least a half dozen jobs—and upon exiting the freeway, Daniel gave up, pocketing his phone.

The streets were broad on the outskirts of the city, and they were empty, thanks to the rain. The bus trundled into the station, and as it did, a group of drivers surrounded the door. Accosting the riders one by one, they asked after their destinations, quoting prices they claimed to be fair, and upon seeing the foreigners, their eyes grew large, like sharks at the smell of blood. Together, Daniel and the Canadians shouldered their way across the lot to where the cabs were all registered, and along the way, Imogen shouted at those who tried to help her with her bags and, at one point, Christopher for trying to bargain.

Daniel followed their cab until they turned at the river—the Xiangjiang browner than he remembered—and under an overpass, his driver stopped to get out and light a cigarette and urinate in the weeds. He was a quiet man, and since Daniel was too, they passed the rest of the ride in silence, speaking only to give directions. Daniel tried calling Neil again, but again there was no answer, so he went to Walking Street, the only place he knew, and bought McDonald's while he waited for news.

It was crowded, since it was the weekend, and the construction made it worse. The area had been excavated to make way for a subway, and there was nowhere to walk. He found a spot with excellent vantage atop the footbridge spanning the road, its railings lined with women sporting umbrellas, their lashes false, the size of dimes. Next to him, a girl was hawking vegetable peelers, like many others on the bridge, and their faces were covered over with slices of cucumber, like adherents of some cult. Daniel waited and ate his hamburger, tracking the look of the clouds above, anxious to get inside and out of his clothing and on with the night that lay ahead.

At last, Neil sent him a message saying that he was sorry and where to meet and that he would be at the statue in fifteen minutes—half an hour, at most. Daniel sighed, moving down to the plaza, and waited with his hands in the pouch of his sweatshirt at the head of the street, where the likeness of one of the province's most decorated heroes had been cast in pure bronze. The square was a popular place to meet, and of those with overdue friends, he was not the only one. The Chinese stared at him as they passed, but compared to Ningyuan, this was nothing.

In fact, he was not the only foreigner. Across the plaza, there was a man wearing headphones, standing in front of the escalator that led to McDonald's, and he appeared to be looking directly in Daniel's direction, although it was hard to be sure. In spite of the weather, he had on sunglasses, which, together with his headphones, obscured the bulk of his features, giving off the impression that he was there but also absent, somehow removed from the scene. Daniel nodded, then checked himself, feeling naïve, averting his eyes as if to look for someone, trying to play it cool. Simply because they came from different countries did not mean they owed each other a hello. He had a feeling that the man was watching him, but still he did not turn around.

About twenty minutes later, he heard someone call him from above, as well as a group of students laughing and shouting at the arrival of his friend. When he looked up, he had to do a double take, for the man he saw there was not familiar: a veritable dandy with no beard, dressed in a handsome three-piece suit.

Oi, Neil shouted as he tramped down the stairs. If it ain't Mr. Ningyuan himself. *Haojiubujian*, mate. Sorry to keep you waiting.

Daniel looked him over, studying his clothes, and tried to fight back a smile. This was not the old drinking buddy he had known. Neil was tall and pushing thirty, and the years were apparent in his eyes, and as they stood there, the Chinese stopped to point and stare at him, for he was also pushing three hundred pounds. Previously, Daniel was used to seeing him in tracksuits—Puma, Adidas, Lacoste, Li-Ning—and when Neil saw the way he was looking at him, he smiled, punching him on one arm.

Wuyanyidui ma? Cat got your tongue?

Sorry, said Daniel. I think you've got the wrong guy. I'm looking for a friend of mine. Goes by the name of Neil. Dresses like a student. Drinks like one, too. Glowering, Neil held up both fists, then broke out into a smile, and Daniel retreated, raising his arms. Seriously, though. What's with the getup? I almost didn't recognize you.

You like? Neil straightened his back and adjusted his tie, tugging at the bottom of his lapels. Behind him, a few girls tittered shyly, and at the sound of them, he turned and smiled, waving *ni hao.*

Looking sharp. You work for the government now or something?

Neil laughed. No. But you'd be surprised how much differently people treat you, dressed like this. I'm telling you, it's all about image. Especially here in China.

Still, nice suit like that? You'd think at least it'd include a watch.

Oh, fuck off. I apologized already, didn't I? Overhead, the sky had begun to mist. Neither of them had an umbrella. Stooping down, Neil picked up Daniel's bag and started walking in the direction of the river. We can't all pull off your look, he said snidely. How was the ride?

Same as always. Long. Uncomfortable. Some lady threw up in the aisle. Noodles. It smelled of something awful.

Well, you made it.

Yeah. What about you? Meetings all day?

Yup. I've been working on this joint venture with a couple of Italians that I met in Guangzhou. Just one of many things I've got going on at the moment. Lots of irons in the fire, you know? It's been crazy busy lately.

Busy is good. What's the project?

Well, it's still in the introductory stages. Import/export kind of deal. We've yet to sort out all of the details.

They turned down an alley where several mindless Pomeranians lay panting in the gutter, dressed in clothes, and continued walking to Neil's apartment, a third-story walk-up near the rear. The alley was sided by vacant mah-jongg halls and hair salons packed with beautiful girls, and its name had been written in soft, white limestone by the hand of some child.

You still teaching?

Only part-time. I left Yali last semester, but I've been subbing at this great private training school since June. It's directly opposite my apartment, and they do all of the prep work for you. When it comes down to it, I must be making triple what I was previously, in terms of hourly wage. Plus, the students are all college-age girls, he said, winking. And the receptionist? Whoo! Don't even get me started. The job is any man's dream. Kills me I have to leave.

Why's that?

Another opportunity's come up. Plus, I want to focus more time on that business I was telling you about. Only so many hours in the day.

That sucks. Sounds like the perfect gig.

You think? They proceeded up the stairs, Neil stomping on the lights, the interior cluttered with more graffiti, marks from a basketball, spent butts. On the ground floor, the word PIG had been scribbled in English, and on the second, there was an inscription that called rather unequivocally for the fall of Little Japan. Actually, he said, I have one more meeting today at six. I'm scheduled to teach, though. Any chance you'd be interested in making a few extra yuan?

Daniel stopped on the stairs, eyeing Neil suspiciously. Any man's dream, huh?

I'm telling you—all you have to do is show up. It's a cakewalk from there.

Fine, Daniel said. But you're buying the first round.

———

The training school was located on the eleventh floor of a high-rise, its classrooms set behind walls of glass, and when Daniel stepped off the elevator, two or three students turned to look. What Neil had told him was correct—for the most part, they were female, and on the whole, they were hot—but he tried his best not to gawk too openly as he went across the foyer, approaching the desk. The receptionist was on a phone call, so he waited patiently, filling out a form, trying to think up ways in which he might greet the girl once she finally got off. She was slender and soft-spoken, with lens-less frames and an open blouse, and when she hung up, he knew exactly what to say to her. Gesturing toward her glasses, he handed her his form.

Are you near- or farsighted? he asked.

She studied him briefly. Again, the phone began to ring. Before she could answer, Daniel heard someone come up behind him. The sound of a clipboard being tapped.

You are Daniel, Neil's friend? Thank you so much for your come!

He turned around to the sight of a woman with hair so unkempt that it looked like a nest. She had on lipstick, but it was smudged, as though applied in great haste.

My God, she said. Neil has not told me. Your hair. So terrifying!

Daniel held out his hand and laughed. *Hong yanse bu shi dai-biao xingyun ma?*

Yes. Good luck! Tucking the clipboard under one arm, she stared at him, smiling. Your Chinese is excellent! Almost as good as Neil's. Her palm was clammy to the touch. My name is Angela. I am the scheduler here at HOPE. Thank you very much for arriving early. Most of our substitutes, they are always late.

No problem. Neil has told me a lot of wonderful things about your company. I'm excited to be here.

Really? She led him into an office. More girls at the desks. A foreigner stood near the door, running off copies—presumably prior to a lesson—but Angela did not introduce them. Neil tells me that you are living in the countryside, she said. Upon hearing this, the other foreigner turned to look at him. Is it true?

Yes. I live in a small town called Ningyuan. It's just south of Yongzhou.

It must be very interesting! Opening a filing cabinet, she took out a folder labeled I-4. Here is your today's lesson. All of the directions are in front. Please put it back once you have finished. I will pay you when leaving. She turned around, then stopped. Oh, and one more. We are asking all of the instructors to wear these today. Picking out a Santa hat from a pile of them on the table, she shook it out, then slapped it on his head. Remember, she said, it is most important that you are entertaining the students. Merry Christmas!

Daniel thanked her and found an empty cubicle and sat down and riffled through the sheets. Neil had not been exaggerating one bit: in terms of prep work, there was none. All he had to do was xerox the materials. Getting up, he made his way over to the copier, where the other foreigner was still working. The man did not acknowledge him. Daniel stood there, eyeing the countdown on the monitor. Twelve, eleven, ten . . .

Hey, he finally said. I'm Daniel.

The man glanced up, then looked him over. Then he lifted the platen and removed the original. He stood on the verge of seven feet. When he spoke, Daniel could tell that he was Australian. He had a nervous, excitable energy, and this reminded Daniel of Thomas.

Dave, he grunted. Collecting the sheets from the catch, he put them in order. Then he took off. Daniel stood there, holding the materials he was about to copy in both hands, and watched him go.

The room they gave him was set in one corner—a small cube of glass overlooking the road—and when he got there, two girls were already waiting for him, sitting in front of the whiteboard with their book bags still on. One was prettier than the other. Her name was Zenith, and she was a student at Hunan University, and after introducing themselves in English, Daniel dove right in. First, he reviewed their homework—a letter to the editor of a magazine, whose name, for some reason, the girls found droll—making corrections and writing on the whiteboard to demonstrate the difference between *would* and *will*. The topic was How to Improve Our City, and fourteen new expressions had been asked of the girls, but all Daniel had to do was check them, writing down their scores at the top of the page. A journal had been given to them by HOPE with inspirational quotes on the cover, and there was a space for their teachers to write down feedback on the completion of each class. Most of the notes Daniel saw there were from Neil, but there were plenty of other handwritings, too. By the time they moved on to the bulk of the lesson, they were already well behind schedule.

Daniel read the directions aloud, handing out the sheets he had made earlier, then allowed Zenith and her classmate, whose name he had already forgotten, several minutes to work alone. They sat with their pens at the table, trying to think of what to write, and, after one or two false starts, they started scribbling away in their books. Daniel stood up and went to the window, observing the grayness that was Changsha, the people and cars on Wuyi Boulevard like miniature replicas or so many ants. The exercise was similar to one he had assigned to his students the year before: a declaration of their dreams that used for its model the most oft-quoted lines from that famous speech. Zenith was done after only a few minutes, but it seemed as if her friend still needed more time, so Daniel sat down and reviewed what she had written, underlining the sentences he liked.

When he was finished, he handed the book back to her, then gave his approval in the form of a smile. She was a buxom, raven-haired girl, and her eyes were wide set, like a Japanese. Her classmate was still working. Feeling somewhat pressed for time, Daniel looked down at his watch.

Zenith, he said finally. Why don't you start?

She nodded. Shifting in place, she held up the paper in front of her and cleared her throat. Then, slowly, she began to read. The girl beside her did not look up.

I have a dream. I have a dream that, one day, I will be an airline stewardess. I will travel to many different countries, and I can receive a very high salary. For this reason, I want to study English, and I will not stop until I have mastered the language. In the words of *Li Yang*: Anything is possible! I know that, eventually, I will have a great result.

Nice, Daniel said. I want you to try it again, though. This time, *dasheng yidian'er*. Like you're standing in front of a crowd.

Zenith considered him hesitantly—her eyes like almonds, tapered and sleek—then sat up and repeated what she had written, this time in a louder and more confident voice. Outside their classroom, other students and teachers turned to look, and Daniel could see Angela standing at one of the computer screens, admiring his work. Following the lesson plan's guidance, Daniel helped the girls review where Zenith had been off, then let the other girl tell them about what she had been working on—something about founding an online shop. She had written much more than necessary, and from the sound of it, she liked to hear herself talk, and by the time they had finished correcting it, it was nearly seven o'clock.

Of what little time they had left, Daniel passed out their homework, then wiped down the board and wrote out the instructions,
just so there would be no later confusion. Thanking the girls, he
asked them if they had any more questions. They stared at him and
started to get ready, but they did not put away their books. Zenith
raised her hand.

Yes?

You need to leave us feedback.

Oh, that's right. Sorry—I almost forgot.

It doesn't matter.

Actually, I've never done this before. Would you mind showing me what to do?

Of course. She motioned him over to the table, and along with
her classmate, she led him through the process. To begin, there
were four boxes to measure their effort, then a short-answer space
to talk about where they could improve. Near the bottom, a bank
of clouds for words of encouragement. Daniel set to filling them
in. The girls stood to either side of him, watching him as he wrote.

Teacher Daniel, Zenith said. Can I ask you a question?

Sure. Just call me Daniel, though. I'm not much older than
you.

Really? How old?

Guess.

She turned to her classmate. Then, in Chinese, she asked
her how old she thought he was. The girl said thirty-one. Daniel
smiled. He continued to write in their notebooks while the two of
them argued among themselves.

Thirty-three, she finally said.

Daniel feigned as if he was hurt. I'm only twenty-four!

The girls blushed. By way of recovery, Zenith told him he
looked mature.

That's OK. Anyway. What was your question?

Oh, yes. I was only wondering: When did you discover your dream of becoming a teacher? We think you are an excellent one!

Here, it was Daniel's turn to blush, both due to the compliment they had extended as well as the assumption they had made. Actually, he said, I'm still not sure I would call this my dream.

What? But you must!

Don't get me wrong—I like it. It's just that, sometimes, it feels like I'm meant for something else.

Such as?

That's the million-dollar question.

The other girl did not understand the expression. Zenith turned and explained it to her, and this caused her to laugh. How long has he been working at HOPE? she asked.

With a smile, Daniel answered in Chinese.

Both girls were taken aback. As if talking to a child, they began to coo and praise his Mandarin. It was patronizing, Daniel supposed, but in a way, he kind of liked it.

So, you will not be teaching us next week?

No. That will probably be Neil or someone else.

Oh . . .

What's the matter? You don't like Neil?

The girls considered each other obliquely. To be honest, Zenith said, he is not the best teacher. After a pause, her classmate nudged her. Besides, she went on, we think you are more handsome.

Me?

Zenith nodded. She was too embarrassed to say anything else. Closing her book, Daniel handed her his comments, and as she read what he had written, her face went red. On a separate piece of paper, she wrote down her number. Hiding it from her classmate, she slid it across the desk.

Angela met Daniel in the office and paid him his wages in cash, asking him what his plans were for the holiday as she walked him out. When they got to the elevators, she handed him her business card. All the front said was HOPE. We really wish that you can come back, she said. The spring term will bringing many new students.

I'd love to, he said, but unfortunately, I'm headed back to Ningyuan on Monday.

Well, let me know if you're ever in town. We often have openings in the summer. The elevator arrived, and they said their goodbyes. Just as the doors were about to close, Angela held up her clipboard and started waving it over her head. Don't forget to call us! she said. Here at HOPE, we're always looking to hire the native Americans!

———

They started that night drinking at Neil's apartment, shooting Ballantine's on the couch, Neil debriefing him on the lesson and every girl who had been in the office. He had a case of Belgian beer that he had imported by way of a friend, and he was insistent about using the correct glassware, displayed on a shelf above his bed. Even though he was dressed in the same suit as that afternoon, he seemed to have lost a bit of his swagger, for all around him, the place was a mess. Shirts hung rough-dried from the ceiling, trousers lay open on the floor, and inside the sunroom, there was a suitcase filled with blankets and all of his more ponderous winter clothes. Food containers crowded the table. While they drank, Neil walked around the apartment, filling a garbage bag by hand. To his credit, he was cleaning up, but this was only in case he succeeded at the bar and ended up bringing a girl back.

By the time they left, Daniel was already drunk, but Neil had brought along beers for the walk. They slugged the bottles casually, strolling the alleyway like cats, Neil unwrapping a pack of Hao Rizi and scrapping the plastic in the street. By then, the salons were filled with women—all of them beautiful, mascaraed, petite—and as they walked past each door, Neil slowed, cursing himself quietly.

Along the curb, men sat on scooters, smoking cigarettes and trading jokes, waiting to spirit the girls, once they were ready, off to whatever crowded parlors, whatever empty rooms.

The city was just now awakening. Neon lights, the scraping of woks. The acrid smell of soy-charred tofu, rising in clouds above the carts. Neil pushed through the crowd with great purpose, like a businessman headed to work, forcing Daniel to hurry after him, brushing past the shoulders of others to keep up. They crossed to the south side of West Liberation where the traffic was heaviest— the taxis and buses at a crawl—and stood in line at an ATM near the entrance to Walking Street. The whole way over, Neil had been talking up the bar.

It's completely different than the last time you were here, he said. They've got a roof deck and everything. Probably closed now, though. You'll have to visit again in the spring.

I don't think I've been to this one before. What's the name?

Fox Bar. Are you sure? It's probably the most popular place for foreigners in the city.

In that case, definitely not. We used to go to the one across the street from where you bought weed, remember? Second on the right when you walk in. What was it called? *Xian Ge*?

Neil smiled. Music-In. He looked nostalgic. I haven't been there in ages.

How about it, then? For old time's sake.

Bu xing.

Why not?

The crowd's not—how shall I say?—conducive.

To what?

Neil considered him as if he were stupid. C'mon now, mate. Do you really have to ask?

Daniel smiled. *Liaojie.* In that case, how about going to meet up with Imogen and Christopher across the river? They're at a party at Lushan.

White girls? Neil frowned. *Xiexie, bu yao.*

I thought you said that this bar we're going to is full of foreigners.

I did. But the main reason I want to go there is that it attracts loads of local girls.

Daniel stood there, shaking his head. You're a dirty old man.

Don't act like you're above it. I'm telling you, tonight is going to be fun. They're throwing a beach-themed party. Hopefully all of the women dress appropriately.

By this point, they had made it to the front of the line. Stepping up to the machine, Neil set his beer on the ledge. With his cigarette dangling from his lips, he fished through his pockets for his card.

You go to this place often? Daniel asked.

Often enough. He punched in his password, then navigated through the options on the screen. Briefly, Daniel caught a glimpse of his balance, and when he did, the amount he saw there shocked him. Apparently, Neil had even less money than he did.

Well, he said, averting his eyes. I'm excited.

Good. The only thing about this place is the owner.

What about him?

He's always pretending like he doesn't know me.

Daniel smiled, raising one eyebrow. God forbid.

You'll see. It's obvious. Pisses me off.

He took out his cash and stuffed it into his wallet. They cut down Walking Street, carried by the surge of pedestrians, pressed up close against the buildings by the ongoing construction. Looking down at his feet, Daniel let Neil do the blocking. At one point, the two of them had to squeeze into a store because the way was too tight, but once they had yielded, the other side just kept coming, making it impossible to get through. Eventually, Neil grew impatient. Lifting his arms, he bulled his way forward.

In time, they came out into a plaza that marked the middle of the strip. Among the crowd, there were women selling hamsters, palming them roughly like chicks, as well as a pair of girls running up to young couples with flowers offered in their hands. Overhead, a gaudy electric sign that would have given an epileptic fits. There were so many people, and as Daniel stood there surveying the scene, a beggar approached them and asked him for money, holding out his hand. In Chinese, Neil lied, telling him they had nothing, then turned to Daniel and hazed him on. Together, the two of them departed across the square.

Just before they got to Hualongchi, it started raining—hard. Above the alley, there were various beer signs, and they walked beneath them for cover. Unsurprisingly, the bar they were going to was all the way in the back. For such a narrow, seedy passage, Daniel was always surprised by how vibrant it was, like the inside of a pinball machine or curio shop, certain streets in Hong Kong. By the time they were out of the weather, Daniel was soaked from head to toe. He wrung out his hair, then followed Neil inside, bellying up next to him at the bar.

The owner's wife was dressed in a bikini that was made out of coconut shells and grass. She was an older woman, but she had an attractiveness to her yet. Neil ordered a couple of beers from her in Chinese, and once they had been served, she hung a garland around each of their necks. Her husband was at the register, and when he saw them, he smiled. Picking up his stein, he came over to greet them. He stank of cigarettes and beer.

Huanying, boys. His accent was terrible. Neil, right?

Hi, Jon.

Merry Christmas!

Likewise. This is my mate. He's visiting from out of town.

The man turned and smiled, looking Daniel over. He wore an enormous pair of mustaches and a drooping felt cap. Welcome to the Middle Kingdom, he said. My name's Jon. I own the place.

Daniel. It's nice meeting you.

Actually, Neil added, Danny here lives in Hunan.

Oh yeah? Whereabouts?

Ningyuan.

The owner drank from his beer, then let out a long, resonant belch. Never heard of the place, he said.

It's near the border with Guangdong. Not too far from Yongzhou.

The owner nodded, but from his expression, Daniel could tell he had not heard of Yongzhou, either. All of a sudden, out of nowhere, he assumed a serious look. Placing his mug on the counter, he pointed at the flowers around their necks.

Whoa, now. What's the big idea? Did the two of you get lei'd by my wife? Upon hearing his own joke, he burst out laughing. It was clear that he had been using the same line all night. So as not to be rude, Daniel and Neil smiled, then turned to look at his wife. She was standing beside him behind the bar, but apparently she did not speak English. Her husband lit a cigarette, then drained what was left in his glass. I always knew that she was a slut!

Eventually, they excused themselves and went upstairs, protecting their beers, the stairway littered with garbage and pony kegs, a deck of scattered cards. There were boxes on the landing of the third floor as well as a button that read, in English, PUSH HERE FOR SERVICE. The floor was packed wall-to-wall with guests. Neil led him over to an open table. On it, in the wood, someone had carved FANTASIES ARE AWESOME.

There was a girl in cat ears behind him who spoke pretty good English as well as a Welshman Neil seemed to know who kept telling everyone how drunk he was. The girl and her friends were all gorgeous. Sitting down, Neil stared at them across the table.

Goddamn it, he said. I'm horny.

Daniel laughed. Well, looks like we've come to the right place. Remind me never to doubt you again.

Neil raised his beer. Cheers, mate. Absentmindedly, they touched rims.

How'd the meeting go earlier?

Hmm? Oh. Quite well. Thanks. I think we're going to be moving forward soon. I should be starting next month.

Congratulations. What's the job?

It's a growing consumer electronics company. External batteries, keyboards—that sort of stuff.

Daniel waited for Neil to continue. At times, he had a sidelong way of answering, as if he were not being truthful. Behind him, an old pair of cowboys was playing foosball, replete with wide-brim hats and all. Neil wiped his nose, then looked down at the wood. He started thumbing through his phone.

What are you going to be doing for them?

Officially? Heading up their overseas department.

All right. What about actually?

Actually? Well, that's the best part. In terms of the day to day, my responsibilities are going to be next to nothing.

Daniel looked at him. How's that?

All they want is a white guy in the office, in case a client stops by to visit. They're called face jobs. Never heard of them?

No. Daniel sat up, drinking pensively from his mug. Really? All you have to do is sit there?

Well, no. Not exactly. There will be meetings, of course. Perhaps a conference or two later in the year. They assured me, however: any involvement I have will be minimal. At most, all I'll be doing is giving speeches or drinking with clients. You know the deal. It ought to give me the time and money to get my own business started. That's the reason I want to do it.

How much are they going to pay you?

Neil mumbled a figure, but, given the noise in the bar, Daniel could not hear him. He leaned across the table.

How much?

Five thousand.

What? You've gotta be kidding me. That's more than twice what I make teaching, just to sit there and do nothing!

Slyly, Neil grinned. Oh, and did I forget to mention? It's in euros. Not renminbi.

He burst out in laughter, then guzzled from his mug, slapping the table. As Daniel cursed him, an older woman sidled up behind him. For a Caucasian, she was not very tall, and she looked somewhat insecure for her years. She had bangles on her forearms. When her eyes came into contact with Daniel's, she raised one finger to her lips. Daniel smiled, but he did not say anything. So as not to ruin the surprise, he drank from his mug.

The woman covered Neil's eyes with her hands and, whispering into one ear, told him to guess. At first, Neil just sat there, grinning like a fool. When he heard the sound of her voice, however, he seemed to deflate. At least he didn't freak out like Thomas, Daniel thought. He rattled off a series of names, then eventually gave up. Clearly disappointed, the woman let go of his face.

It's Jan, she said.

Jan. Of course! Sorry, I didn't recognize your voice. Softening his tone, Neil gave her a concerned look. You're not sick, are you?

No. I don't think so. She seemed moved that he would worry about her. Sliding in closer, she took one of Neil's cigarettes, then sat down and threw one leg over his lap in a ribald gesture. Then she turned to Daniel. Who's your friend?

Introductions were made, and for the second time that hour, Daniel had to explain where he was from. He could tell that Jan had a thing for Neil, but unless he was wrong, she was making eyes at him, too. He asked her where she was from.

Minnesota.

Really? I work with a guy from Saint Paul.

In Ningyuan?

Daniel nodded. His name is Thomas. He used to live in Changsha.

Wait a minute—Thomas Guillard?

Again, Daniel nodded. Warily this time. You know him?

You bet I do. We used to work together. He just disappeared after last term. What a miserable old lout! I had to teach all of his classes till the school found a replacement.

You work at Yali?

She looked at him, then at Neil. Then she laughed. Yali Middle School? No. This was at *Yangguang You'eryuan*. Daniel winced at her butchering of the pronunciation. It's on Wuyi Boulevard, near the station. I just started my own yoga studio, though. That's what I do now. Turning, she poked Neil in the gut. Actually, I could use your help getting this one to sign up. He could afford to lose a few.

Neil ignored her. I remember him. Old guy, with a limp? He used to come in here a lot, I think. Jon is pretty good friends with him.

Daniel nodded. Turning to Jan, he put down his mug. A kindergarten, you said?

Yeah. Why? Don't tell me he told you he used to teach at Yali. Not just me, our school. I can't believe they never checked.

Jan sighed, rolling her eyes. Oh, China, she said.

Again, Daniel winced. Any idea why he left?

No. Like I said, he completely blindsided us. He wasn't the best teacher, though. It was probably a blessing in disguise. Sorry to hear that you got stuck with him.

Daniel shrugged. The three of them killed their beers, then pushed the button and waited for the server and ordered more. Jan invited them to her table, but Neil only went so far as to say that they would be over soon. A hulking local who had been chatting with the cowboys came over and offered them both a smoke, carrying his own bottle of vodka, his own bottle of juice, and, when the waiter returned, ordered a round of shots for the two of them, claiming that he was already drunk. Although his English was as good as fluent, they spoke predominantly in Mandarin throughout. From Neil, Daniel learned that he had recently beaten leukemia. Not half a year past. Still, he smoked like a chimney.

When the shots finally arrived, Daniel sat there, studying them in awe. They had been layered alternately in red and green for Christmas, and they were set in paper cups.

Jell-O shots? he said. Now I've seen everything.

Neil laughed. I've a feeling we're not in Ningyuan anymore.

They played Liar's Dice, then Indian Poker, then Fuck the Dealer, then Circle of Death. By the time they looked up to order, Daniel was blotto, but so was everybody else. The cards had been provided by the bar, and on them were naked pictures of Asian women as well as profanities written in English, scribbled in Italian, drawn in French. It was hard to hear each other, and this seemed to annoy their new friend. He had to shout at them whenever he wanted to talk. Still, it was almost impossible to follow what he said.

Niurou, he repeated at the top of his lungs. Beef! Getting up, he adjusted his shirt, then pointed at the stairs. Toilet!

Daniel watched him walk away, lighting one of Neil's cigarettes using the candle on the table between them, then sat back, exhaling a thin line of smoke through the haze of the room. Neil was deep in conversation with the cowboys and some girl, and although he could have easily moved around to join them, he did not. With about three fingers left in his beer, he hailed the waiter and ordered another, then listened to the Welshman at the table behind them call the boy over, just for fun. As Daniel sat there, listening to the man give the kid a hard time, someone tapped him on the shoulder. It was the girl wearing cat ears. When Daniel acknowledged her, she blushed.

You speak Mandarin so well, she said. When I heard you, I thought that you were a Chinese.

Nali ya, he said.

Are you a student here?

No. Actually, I'm Chinese.

She laughed. When did you start studying?

In college. I took it for four years.

Four years, and it's already so good? Impossible!

Daniel leaned over and whispered into her ear. Honestly, he said. It's pretty bad. I don't know why, but I can only speak fluently when I'm talking to pretty girls.

Again, she blushed. Daniel asked her if she wanted a drink, but before she could answer, Neil came over and interrupted them, telling the girl that he had almost worn the same set of ears that night. She seemed to find this funny. Spinning around on her stool, she gave him hers, and as Neil posed in the aisle, she showed her friends and took a few pictures, the Welshman mocking him between drags on his cigarette, ignoring Daniel. He had an unfortunately thuggish look. In time, Neil and Daniel had worked their way onto the table, and so as to promote a sense of camaraderie, Daniel ordered shots of Jäger for the group. After they downed it, he nodded and introduced himself to the others, but the Welshman just sat there, glaring at him. He spat beneath the table.

I hear your Chinese is pretty good.

There was an edge to his voice. Taken off guard, Daniel looked him straight in the eyes.

It's all right, I guess.

I don't think I've seen you in here before. He ran his eyes over Daniel's ears, his arms, his hair. Then he laughed. I'd remember you.

Daniel looked at Neil, but Neil was too busy flirting with the girls. He turned back to consider the man.

Well, that would make sense, seeing as I don't live in Changsha.

Didn't think you did.

Daniel frowned. Do you have some sort of problem with me?

The man lit a new cigarette, then ashed it into his mug. What do you do? Wait, let me guess. A teacher? The question was dripping with condescension.

As a matter of fact, yes. You have something against teaching?

The man shrugged. He picked up an imaginary object and presented it to the table. WATER, he drawled, loudly. Either because he was drunk or trying to act like a fool, he spoke like a moron, distinguishing each syllable. JUICE, he continued. The girls regarded him uncomfortably, staring down into their cups, like tea readers. He pointed to a spot on the table in front of Daniel. APPLE. BANANA. Seriously, he said. The job is an absolute joke.

His act had drawn Neil's attention, and as Daniel bridled, the Welshman sat back, smiling complacently, then waved for their server. When the boy approached, he told him what he wanted so quickly that even Daniel would have been hard pressed to follow. The boy stood there, squinting in frustration, until Daniel finally repeated what he had said in Chinese. He stared the man down, trying to contain his anger. And what is it, exactly, that you do? he asked.

I'm a writer.

Where?

A Hong Kong–based travel magazine. I'm moving back home tomorrow, though. Going to be working for a paper. You know, starting the rest of my life. Tonight's the big send-off.

Good riddance, Daniel said.

The man sat up and cocked one of his eyebrows, as if somehow Daniel had been mincing his words. There was an awkward moment of silence, until finally Neil stepped in. He cleared his throat, chuckling nervously.

Whoa, now. Let's all just take it easy, all right? Kayden's good people. Turning to Kayden, he smiled. So is Daniel. He raised his glass and urged them to follow. We're all friends here, yeah? Cool. All right, *ganbei*.

The three of them drank. Once they were finished, Daniel stood up and excused himself from the table. He headed back down to the bar. He was in the process of paying for another beer when Neil crept up beside him. His tie was unraveled, and his shirttails were coming untucked.

Don't worry about that guy, he said.

Who's worried?

He's just drunk. That's all. It's his last night in-country.

Daniel took a sip from his beer so that the foam would not run over, then, simply out of habit, left a tip on the bar. Like a croupier, Neil raked it back.

Whatever. He's sure got one hell of a chip on his shoulder, though.

You know how it is. Everybody wants to think they're the only foreigner living in China.

Daniel considered this for a moment. I guess.

The owner's wife came over and set down Neil's drink on the counter. Winking at her puckishly, he shrugged. C'mon, mate. The night's not half over. Those *meinüs* looked like they were into us.

What about Jan?

Don't start. To be honest, she's been after me for weeks. For the life of me, I can't remember where or when we met, though. I must have been drunk. Anyways, I've always wanted to get with a girl in cat ears. Sexy, no?

An amused smile crossed Daniel's face. I never pegged you for a furry.

There's a lot you don't know about me. Just follow my lead, OK?

By the time they returned upstairs, the scene had devolved into total debauchery. People were puking out of the windows onto Hualongchi below, and at one point, a man old enough to be Daniel's father fell over backward in his chair and, looking like he was on Queer Street, had to be carried outside by his friends. They led him supportively, talking to him like a child. Daniel and Neil spoke with the girls, but Daniel was not in the right mood, and after excusing himself again, he went back downstairs to the bathroom, avoiding their table upon his return. He did a lap around the room. In the back, there was a game of cards going on in one corner, led by a giant Romanian who sat smoking a joint, and after a while, a space opened up at the table next to him. Daniel sat down and drank and studied his cards, eyeing the Welshman through the crowd, and after an hour or two, he had doubled his initial stack, thanks to a string of lucky hands. Glancing up, he noticed that Neil and the girls were gone. Ten minutes, he announced to the others. His opponents grumbled, but no one objected in the end.

He stopped for shaokao on his way back home to Neil's apartment. The rain was falling lightly overhead, the cobblestones slick from the mixture of water and vomit that grouted their crevices, like mud. There were several boys waiting in front of the cart with him, smoking their cigarettes in a circle, as well as an old crone selling neon glow sticks, inflatable hammers, artificial roses, Mylar balloons. While they waited for their food, she beat them playfully over the head, her smile warm, but also uncanny—an empty rictus of gums. Daniel tried calling Neil's phone, but, as expected, there was no answer. He ate his meal at the head of the alley, feeling miserable and drunk.

Neil did not come to the door right away when he knocked, so Daniel waited for a few seconds in the hallway, then he knocked again. He was just about to give up when he heard the inner door crack. Neil stood shirtless and breathing heavily, and, good lord, was he fat, his collarbone flushed, his nipples erect, an angular bulge in his pants. Something wild and unfamiliar about his look. Inside, a pile of bangles lay on the floor. Daniel could hear someone behind the door, rustling in bed.

Gingerly, Neil crept outside. It was frigid in the hall, but he did not seem to care.

I'm a little busy right now, mate.

I can see that. It's just—I've got nowhere else to go.

Neil frowned and hitched up his pants. We should have thought about this earlier.

How much longer do you need?

Not sure. We just got started. I'd say an hour, at least.

Daniel groaned. Neil reached inside the door and retrieved his cigarettes. Here, he said. Take 'em.

Gee, thanks.

Better yet, go ahead and book yourself a room. I'll pay you back for it tomorrow.

You sure?

Absolutely. This way, everybody's comfortable. Just don't go crazy, yeah? Call me in the morning when you wake up. We'll get lunch.

I will, if you'll answer your phone.

Done.

With that, he closed the door. Daniel stood in the hallway for a moment, smoking a cigarette, until at last he heard the sound of Neil's bedframe begin to squeak and buck against the wall. A mundane thwacking of flesh. Chewing his lip, he went back down the stairs the way he had come up. Given the hour, the streets were abandoned, but all of the buildings were still lit.

He walked down Wuyi Boulevard, among the banks and hotels, then crossed the road and headed north, dragging his feet. Even though he was tired, he realized as soon as he stepped outside that he was not yet ready to go to sleep. He wandered aimlessly, like a vagrant, following Furong Lu, until he came to a crossroads in his heart. The streets grew wider, longer, and lonelier the farther he went.

After a while, it started raining again. He found a bus stop and sat in the darkness, looking for a taxi, but there were none. By that point, he had begun to doubt himself, and the waiting did not help.

A pair of dogs appeared on the curb, standing ass to ass beneath a magnolia tree, from which diodes of almost every imaginable color hung, turning in the wind, like Spanish moss. When Daniel eyed the dogs, they growled, and at that moment, he felt like the only person left on earth. And yet, somehow, this sense of loneliness made him feel important. It would be another thirty minutes until a taxi came by.

When the driver spotted him, he pulled a U-turn, then drove through the water and rolled down the glass. He was a slender man of thirty, with narrow eyes, crooked teeth.

Dao nali ya? he asked.

Yao dapao.

The driver looked at him but gave no reaction. He turned away from the window, then checked the rearview mirror and nodded. *Shang,* he said. Daniel got in.

The ride seemed to last forever—how far had he walked? Daniel offered him one of Neil's cigarettes, but the man did not smoke. They drove in silence and listened to the radio, the rain like a hand on the car's roof, and followed the road as it dipped underneath the expressway, at which point they came to a light. The driver leaned forward and wiped condensation from the glass, then pointed across the intersection. *Nali,* he said. *Kan.*

The girls sat on cheap, plastic stools, framed by the door, and when they saw the car pull up, they set down their phones, craning to look. The shop was lit by a dim purple bulb, reflected in pools on the sidewalk, and it was the only hair salon still open down the length of the block.

Laowai, they whispered excitedly as Daniel walked in. He lowered his hood and looked them over, smiling at the ones he liked. They were clothed in tawdry dishabille. Behind them, a middle-aged woman, dressed more modestly, sat watching TV. She stood at the sound of his arrival. Corded muscles braided her neck.

Ni shi na guo ren? she asked.

Daniel told her that he was Canadian. All of the girls started murmuring, as if they had heard of—but never been with—this kind before. The madam nodded and gestured to both sides, instructing him to pick.

For the most part, they were pretty, but only one of them was what you would call beautiful. Daniel approached her and held out a hand. Almost at once, the other girls lost interest. From the way they reacted, he could tell this was often the case. The madam told him the going rate for foreigners, then, once she had been paid, returned to her seat. They went out through a door in the back of the room, up a narrow flight of stairs.

Like everyone else, the girl asked him what his reasons were for coming to China. Daniel gave her the standard answer, which he had been practicing now for months. She praised his Chinese, then asked him about his country—what was it like?—but now that he was alone with her, he could no longer lie. He told her that he was an American. When the girl heard this, she grew panicked and, in a high-pitched, whiny voice, begged him to take it out, but Daniel just smiled, assuming this to be part of some act intended to please him. After a while, however, he realized the girl was not acting. She started tugging at his belt. According to what she had heard, Americans were well-endowed, and as she stood there trying to get his pants off, other girls in other stalls with other johns called out. The walls stopped just shy of the ceiling, and as a result, you could hear everything: shouting, grunting, slaps. A tired, rhythmic chant. Daniel told her that he had to go to the bathroom, but this did not seem to discourage her. He had to shoulder the door shut just to keep her out. It was then, for the first time all night, he realized he was soaked.

The room was a cubbyhole, little more. A wall-to-wall mattress, little else. He lay down and removed his sneakers as the girl climbed over him, and before he knew it, she was undressed. She lay down next to him. Still fretting, unbuttoning his clothes. She had enormous breasts and large teeth and tufts of hair beneath her arms, and when Daniel felt the warmth of her skin against him, he finally relaxed. It was soft and smooth and natural, and there was hardly any muscle to it at all. Gaping at his tattoos, she ran a finger across his chest, then squeezed his biceps and told him how hard it was, playing with the hair at his waist. She followed it down, farther and farther, until it vanished into his pants, and once she had finally got him naked, she looked up and smiled, folding his clothes. Daniel smiled back. Setting his belongings at the bottom of the mattress, she removed a condom from her purse, then began to unroll it between her fingers. Lowering her head down onto his shoulder, she told him she was no longer scared.

八

Guillard passed that night tossing and turning and covered in sweat and awoke the next morning with a pain in his bladder and no dreams. The first thing he noticed was that he had forgotten to draw the blinds. It had been raining all night, judging from the state of the courts, and it was likely to continue falling all day, given the color of the sky. He had five or six different space heaters going, which he kept running around the clock, but they were all being neutralized at the moment, for he had forgotten to close the door. He rolled out of bed and, steeling himself, went to the bathroom across the hall. Hunan had nothing on Minnesota. Still, it was a different sort of cold.

The water seeped into everything, and, once wet, it was hard to get dry. Guillard's clothing lay in a pile on the floor, next to an empty bottle of beer. His first inclination was to smoke something, but then he remembered he was out of cigarettes. Clambering back into bed, he thought about what had happened the night before.

It had only been the third time he had gone out since the incident at the pool hall, and despite that he had waited until it was dark outside, the Chinese had still noticed him at the register, trying to pay for his things. Apparently, word had gotten out. A crowd had gathered before he knew it, calling him foreign devil, blocking the door, and on account of their presence there, the cashier had refused to accept his money. They would not even let him explain. Guillard had been forced to leave his food on the scanner and lurch back, empty-handed, through the rain.

The others had left on Saturday morning without informing him of their plans. By that point, Guillard was used to being excluded. He had known many others like them in Changsha: idealistic and full of intention, but also, in a way, fooling themselves, naïve. A kid like Daniel would never understand anything about life and its limitations or just how pointless it all was. His sense of purpose was shallow and misguided, and just like some kind of idiot, he wore it flamboyantly from his sleeve. He reminded Guillard of himself at that age, and the less he had to see of him, the better. Especially around the holidays.

By one thirty, he was starving, but he stayed in bed, debating whether or not to go downstairs. Aside from the beer and a week-old container of eggplant, there was nothing in the fridge. He was just about to settle for the leftovers when someone started knocking on his door.

As a general rule, Guillard tended to avoid callers, but since he had been holed up inside of his apartment all week, he got up to see. Greeting the cold, he limped down the hallway, donning his robe, then sidled up next to the peephole, bugging one eye. Mr. Cai had been on him about electricity since Tuesday, and during that time, he had been over twice already to tell him to turn it down. Guillard held his breath, balanced on the balls of his feet, and squinted through the glass.

It was a girl, dressed in heels, but she was standing in front of Daniel's door, not his. There was something else on the landing at her feet, but Guillard could not tell what it was. She began to strike the door again, using the bottom of her fist, then gave up and taped a piece of paper under the peephole. Then she stepped back. There was something alluring about her hair. Guillard pressed closer, trying to get a better look, but as he did, he heard a sound—the frame of the door against his weight.

Bella turned and looked right at him. Her face was distorted in the glass.

Mr. Thomas? she said. Is that you?

He stood there, not saying anything, like a deer caught in the headlights. Finally, seeing no other option, he opened the door.

Merry Christmas, Bella said.

You, too.

She stood on the landing, wet from the hatch, between two bags of fruit the size of basketballs. She had discarded her uniform for a skirt and tights, and although she had an umbrella, her shoulders were drenched. She had always had short hair—it was one of the policies of the school—but she had altered it somehow, reshaping the cut and the volume. The bangs. There was still a thin, purple bruise across one of her cheeks, and along with her birthmark, it gave an odd sort of symmetry to her face.

How are you? he asked.

Fine. And you?

No, I mean, how's your face?

Oh. It's getting better. I've been eating some medicines every night.

Guillard nodded, but he was confused. Out of everyone in Ningyuan, she seemed the least upset by what he had done.

You know, he said, awkwardly, there's something I've been meaning to tell you.

Yes?

Well, the thing is—I hope you know that, what happened, it was an accident.

She looked at him for a moment, then bowed her head, brushing it off.

It doesn't matter. I know you didn't mean to. Besides, I should not have surprised you like that. I was just excited, that's all.

You aren't mad at me?

Of course not. After all, today is Christmas.

Guillard looked at her for a moment. Then he pointed at the fruit.

You carry all of that up here by yourself?

Bella laughed. Me? Impossible. I am so weak! Maybe it was Santa. She looked at him ironically and smiled. Have you been naughty this year or nice?

He ignored the question and stepped out into the stairwell to inspect the fruit more carefully. He still had a bag of clementines in the parlor, which had been given to him by the school, but they had been rotting since fall.

Shenme dongxi? he asked.

I don't know how you call them in English, but the Chinese name is *youzi.*

Any good?

I don't like them, but my father thinks they are delicious. Would you like my help bringing them in?

He nodded and stepped out of the way and watched her fight the bag over the sill. There was another one for Daniel, and Guillard could not help but notice how much fuller than his it was. An antithetical couplet framed the boy's door, while below it, a few joss sticks rose from a jar. Both jambs were coated with handbills. Sundry, apotropaic herbs. From the exterior, it had to be one of the most Chinese-looking apartments on campus.

Put them over there, he said. Next to the oranges, ya?

Bella dragged the fruit across the floor, then propped it against the wall. Once she had finished, she turned around. Almost immediately, she blushed.

Mr. Thomas. Please, take care . . .

Guillard looked down at himself. His robe was tied negligently around his waist—that much was true—but other than that, all you could really see was his chest. Not even the nipples, at that. Folding the lapels dutifully, one over the other, he cinched them tight. There, he said. How's that?

Bella nodded. Aren't you cold?

This is nothing. There's probably a foot of snow on the ground back home where I'm from. Don't get me wrong—I hate the rain. But I'd take it over snow any day.

Bella started going through his stuff. She picked up a tchotchke one of Guillard's Chinese colleagues had given him and turned it over in the light. It was a painted wooden cottage, with several rows of fence line attached to the base, meant to be used for holding mail—an utter piece of crap. If there was one thing the Chinese were bad at, it was giving gifts. Bella seemed to like it, however. Do you know where everyone else is? she asked.

Guillard went over and took it away from her, then set it back down on the shelf. Changsha, he told her. Why? You need them?

Nothing. I just wanted to wish them a Merry Christmas. Last year, we had a party in the English library. We had a—how do you call it?—Yankee swap. Yes, that's right. Teacher Daniel dressed up like Santa. He even went out to the countryside and cut down a tree!

Guillard rolled his eyes. He knew about the party she was talking about, since the decorations were still up. Dusty garlands, wreaths, tinsel. A desiccated sapling, choked in lights. The room had the look of a sepulcher, and something about that made him happy, although he could not say what.

Well, sorry to let you down, but it seems like he forgot about you this year. Come back again later, ya? No parties here.

He started herding her toward the door. Bella was looking around the apartment, however, concerned about the mess. There were boots and shoes along the baseboard and empty bottles, a bag of trash, and, in the kitchen, a stack of dishes in one of the wash-tubs about two feet high. It looked like some kind of middle school science experiment. Every available object had been used for an ashtray, and nowhere was rid of the smell of butts. Bella seemed to be considering him anew. There was a pity in that look.

Maybe, she said, if you are interested, we can celebrate together. After all, I ought to spend Christmas with an American. That's why you are here.

Is it, now.

Yes, to be building a bridge between our two cultures.

Guillard sighed. I'll pass. It's the weekend. I'm tired, and I'm hungover. I haven't eaten anything all day. Come back again later, ya? I'm sure Daniel will be happy to hang out with you then. Anyway, Christmas is a scam. It doesn't matter when you celebrate it. Especially here, in China. It's lost its original meaning.

But Teacher Daniel . . .

I don't care about Teacher Daniel. I'm going back to bed once I dig up something to eat. Merry Christmas, he said. Thanks again for the fruit.

He closed the door and stood there quietly and waited for her to leave, but she did not go. After a moment, like a Jehovah's Witness, she started knocking again.

Mr. Thomas? Are you still there? I'll cook you dinner, if you want. I can go down and buy some groceries, now. Give me an hour, OK? Don't worry, it will be delicious—I promise!

Guillard opened the door. All right, he said. Just hang on a minute. I'll write you up a list.

———

Bella returned with a bag full of vegetables and salted peanuts and a live duck. The bird hung upside down from its ankles—quiet, for the most part—hyperventilating in the stairwell, as if it knew what was coming. It smelled of bird shit and water and feathers, and there were corpuscles around its mouth—large, unsightly red protuberances that, in their placement, were not all too dissimilar from Bella's mark. Guillard considered the bird uncertainly, then turned to face her, hitching up his pants. Where do you think you're going with that thing? he asked. Not in here, I hope.

Bella ignored him good-naturedly and pushed her way into the apartment. It is for eating, Mr. Thomas. Just wait. I'm going to make you our *Ningyuan* people's specialty: blood duck.

He closed the door and made a face. Sounds delicious.

Have you ever tried it before?

No. I guess there's a first time for everything, though.

She nodded and made her way into the kitchen. Unbinding the bird's legs, she tied it by the same piece of string to the sideboard, then put away the groceries and turned on the stove. The room was so cold that they could see themselves breathing. She opened the cupboards, but they were empty. She went through the sideboard and the refrigerator, but they were both empty, too.

Where is the oil? she asked.

Guillard was hovering in the doorway, like a sneak. I must have run out, if there's none. Check underneath the burner—there's a shelf. That's where I put all of the stuff the last guy left me. You think it's dirty now—you should have seen the place when I moved in.

Bella rose, shaking her head. What about soy?

Sauce? I don't think so.

Vinegar?

Mei you.

With her hands on her hips, she considered him briefly, then flapped her arms and exhaled. Rice? she asked, aghast.

Guillard frowned, shaking his head. I thought you said that you were the one who was going shopping. I'm a teacher, not a grocer.

Still, she said. I was hoping that you would have something. It doesn't matter. I'll go out again. As Teacher Daniel always says, good things are coming to those who wait!

Guillard watched her from his window as she hurried across the courts. The river had flooded the yard, drowning the trees along the bank, and everywhere he looked, the little pathways he took to classes had disappeared and turned to mud. Upriver, a defunct viaduct rose against the mountains, up to its knees in brown sludge, while, closer yet, the cages over the windows on the buildings hung bleeding rust, like a girl's mascara, down their fronts. Lounging in bed, he did nothing, waiting for her return. He brewed a cup of the awful coffee he had bought a long time ago at the store and drank it quietly in front of the window, cursing his luck.

When she came back, she went straight to washing the dishes, so Guillard did not see it necessary to come out of his room. She made a racket in the kitchen, banging pots and dropping pans, and by the time she had finished, there was water all over the floor. Guillard dumped the dregs of his coffee out through the window, then put on his coat and crossed the hall, taking note of the way she had straightened up the living room, the pile of garbage beside the door. She had swept the floor and lined up his sneakers and opened the windows to let in some air and dumped all of his ashes down the toilet, his half-empty bottles down the drain.

She was shaving the duck's neck when he came into the kitchen, the knife moving dexterously in one hand, and she nearly lopped the bird's head off when she heard him sit down. Across the alley, an old woman in a Mao-era jacket watched them expressionlessly from her room, cutting strips of paper, like a bricklayer, sealing off the glass. Bella turned to him and smiled. She asked for help finding a bowl. Guillard opened the cupboard and handed her one, then went through the groceries, looking for food. His neighbor was still watching them. Suspiciously, like a hawk.

How much longer until we eat? He rinsed out his mug and set it to dry and opened the refrigerator, hunting for beer. Two of the bottles were already frozen, but fortunately, one of them was not.

Forty minutes, she said. Go and have a rest, Mr. Thomas. I will call you when it is ready.

He pointed at the duck. I hope you aren't planning on gutting that thing in here.

Yes, but don't worry—I've done it before.

Shit, no. Take it out onto the landing. I don't want you spraying blood all over the floor.

Trust me, it's OK. Killing it out there is too—she struggled for a moment as she searched for the word—impractical. I will leave your kitchen more cleaner than when I found it. *Fangxin!*

Guillard snorted, then reached for the peanuts. He made a smacking sound while he ate. If it annoyed her, Bella did not say anything. She went back to what she had been doing.

She was a merciless cook. With the duck in one arm—its neck folded back, like a trap—she sawed away at the skin with the edge of a razor Guillard realized too late to be his own. She caught the blood in the bowl he had given her without spilling a single drop, then dumped the body—rather unceremoniously—into a washtub next to the sink. As the bird heaved its last breath, Guillard walked over, staring down into the tub, and cringed at what he saw there: the cold, dead eye of the duck, staring back at him. All of a sudden, it jerked.

She took off its feathers and boiled some water, then filled up the washtub and let it soak. As she began to remove the vegetables and organize them, Guillard sat down next to her. Without meaning to, he farted. Bella looked up at him and laughed.

What foods do Americans usually eat on Christmas? she asked. I know that turkey is customary for Thanksgiving, but what about today? Is it bread and wine, or something else?

What makes you think that?

Teacher Daniel told us that Americans eat bread and drink wine to pretend that it is the body of Jesus. I think it is so interesting! You are so superstitious.

Religious, you mean. We only do that when we go to church. It's a kind of ritual, not a meal.

A ritual? What's that?

Guillard sat back and thought about this before replying. It's something important that people do in a certain order, at a certain time. Like the way you always rise and greet me at the beginning of class.

Oh, I know. We have many of those in China. Spring Festival— the Chinese New Year—especially.

I know what Spring Festival is.

Bella nodded and took off her coat. She was wearing a sweater with a yellow face on it, and at the bottom, in English, it said HAPPY SMILE. It was tighter than the polos she normally wore, and for the first time ever, Guillard noticed that she had breasts. She took a carrot out and began to cut it at odd angles. Guillard looked across the alley, but all he could see where the woman had been watching them was a wall of newspaper. Stiffly, he took a pull from his drink.

So, what is it that you eat? she asked him.

Eh?

On Christmas. What is the ritual?

Oh, beats me. Ham, maybe beef. Turkey, sometimes. I don't think there's any one tradition, really. Depends on the family.

What about yours?

Guillard squinted and scratched a mark on the wall. He examined the dirt beneath his nails. As kids, we used to eat liver and onions, he said. We all hated it, but our father insisted. It was his favorite. Our mother would only cook it for him once a year. Too rich, she said. After we were finished, we would watch a movie. Always the same one.

Which one?

It's a Wonderful Life. Over the course of my childhood, I must have watched that movie at least a dozen times.

What is it about?

Guillard looked at her and laughed. When it dawned on him that she was serious, however, his expression grew more concerned.

Don't tell me you've never seen *It's a Wonderful Life* before.

No, I don't think so. Last year, Teacher Daniel let us watch *A Christmas Story* in class. We learned a lot about how to celebrate the holiday in America. And the little boy, Ralphie, he was so cute!

That film's garbage. *It's a Wonderful Life* is one of the most critically acclaimed movies of all time.

Says who?

The critics. Who else?

Do you have a copy?

No. Knowing China, though, you can probably find it online.

Let's watch it later!

All right, just calm down. Maybe. If we can find it.

She smiled and wiped off the blade and raked the carrots into a bowl. What about with your children? she asked. What did you do with them?

Who ever said that I have kids?

No one, I just . . .

It's fine. Just don't start making too many assumptions, ya? I'm gonna head back into my room now and watch TV. Give me a holler when the food's ready. Or, better yet, bring it in. We'll eat in there, where it's warmer.

He watched a program for a little while broadcast from the capital and smoked the cigarettes that Bella had brought him and finished his beer. His head was starting to hurt, but the beer helped. The show was entirely in Chinese, but there were a few good-looking women in the cast, and as Guillard sat there, lusting after them like a teenager, his mind went blank. He drifted off. The smell of Bella's cooking wafted in from across the hall. When she entered, she found him sleeping, and once she had arranged everything, she woke him up. There was a bowlful of vegetables, a small plate of tofu, and, in the center, the duck. It had been braised in its own blood, and he could still see the mandible, but by that point, he was so hungry that he would have eaten anything. Bella handed him a fork. He scooped through the dishes skeptically, prodding at the meat. For a moment, they just sat there, eating quietly. Eventually, Bella asked him what he thought.

It's all right, he shrugged. Mixed with the sauce, the beans aren't half bad. I swear, though, I'll never understand why you people like bones so much. It's almost impossible to eat.

But that's where the flavor is, she said. You really don't like them?

Guillard spit into his napkin, then folded it and set it down on the couch. *Zhen de,* he said. Really. I don't.

At some point, you'll have to come to my grandmother's house. She lives outside of *Ningyuan*. Beyond *Wuligou*. Her food is the best. Mine is just so-so.

Guillard could tell she was looking for reassurance. He got some rice from the pot on the floor, then drizzled it with sauce and shoveled it down his throat. The rice is good, he said between bites. Washing it down with beer, he glanced across the table, then lifted up the glass. You want some? he asked.

OK.

She got a glass, and when she came back, Guillard poured some beer out for her, as one might an expensive wine. She nursed it like tea while she ate. Five minutes later, she was still going on about her grandmother and all of the food the woman could make, until, suddenly, something occurred to her. Clapping excitedly, she set down her rice.

Spring Festival, she said. You can come to visit my grandparents' house then! We can invite the other foreign teachers, too.

My entire family will be there. My parents, my brother, my aunt. My aunt, she is very beautiful.

Guillard was picking at the duck. He found one piece of meat at the bottom of the pile and, without thinking, took it for himself. You're turning into quite a young woman yourself, he said.

Thank you, she said.

Did you say you have a brother?

Yes.

How does that work?

Excuse me?

I thought there was the policy in China. Only one kid per house.

Oh. Well. My parents argued for his birth. The government's official policy is that you can have another child, but only if there is something wrong with your first. Guillard looked at her. My deformity, she said, pointing to her face.

What, that? You can't even notice it. Where I come from, those are called beauty marks, not deformities. This is a deformity, he said, shaking out his leg. Ya?

Bella laughed. Anyway, everyone will be there. That is the ritual in China. I hope you and the other foreigners can come. What a more authentic way to spend the Chinese New Year than with a real Chinese family?

The television was still on. Guillard was watching it, not her. Well, he said, we'll have to see. It's still a long ways off. When is it this year?

The end of next month. We'll have a three-week vacation from school.

We'll see. For now, let's just focus on making it through winter.

Playfully, Bella pouted. As she cleared away the dishes, he poured her more beer. She left the door open on her way to the kitchen, releasing all of the heat that had been accumulating over the course of the afternoon, and, as Guillard watched her bus the table, he felt somehow closer to the girl. She was a nuisance—that much was certain—but he could control her, if need be. He drank some more beer, then reclined, putting up his legs. A man could get used to this, he thought. Screw the suckers back home.

Can we watch the movie now?

She stood framed in the doorway, water running down her arms and, between her thighs, the jacket she had taken off earlier. She was tying back her hair. Outside, the rain was still falling, and despite the fact that it was Sunday afternoon, the bells were still on, blaring the same low, drawn-out dirge across the river, plaintive as doves.

Sure, he said. Just close the door. We don't want to let in the cold.

九

The note had been taped to Daniel's door, just like all of the rest. He had returned on the five o'clock bus from Changsha and not gotten back to campus until midnight. The Canadians were already home—he could see their lights across the courts—and from his apartment, he could hear them arguing, their voices muffled through the floor. He found a bag of pomelos on the landing but left it outside to deal with come morning, then fixed himself a drink and retired for the evening, undressing while he unpacked. When he was done, he read the letter. The handwriting was cramped but ultimately legible.

Dear Teacher Daniel:

I'm very glad that I can get along well with you! In the last two years, We have known many from each other. I like your class very much! And English corner too. Very patient you are. I have known that your lessons are interesting and live. But some time, maybe not. In a word, I just like it!

Please forgive me haven't gone to English corner often since I became a Senior 2 student, because I need to study a lot to make my grade have a great progress. I may have opportunity to go to a good university. When I was a Senior 1 student, I neerly went to English corner everyday. I think it is very good to learn English, but I've less free time now, sorry! If I can, I hope I can stay with you all of the days. What a happy thing it would be. Do you remember I told you my dream: found a mass organization, it can be about teaching or some hobbies. I hope my dream can come true, and I will work hard to make the group more and more big. I can!

I will go to a university in the United States after I graduated from college, if my application for study abroad might be approve. I think America's education is more better than China, education in China is very rigid, study, study, all time, so tired, so, therefore, I need a new retional knowledge of reality and a new way to consider. This is important for me to achieve my dream.

Actually, I've really improved my English a lot from your coming to China. So, As a teacher, you do a good job!

As a friend, however, you did not very well. Because you often overlooked me. I just say hello to you. But you cannot hear me. I'm so sad.

But it's OK! I know you're busy. In the future, I still want that, even you overlook me. But time isn't a good boy. The school year is already halfway.

Will you be staying for another year? I hope so. Next year, I will graduating, and it would be my dream that you could be there. I can always remember you play the guitar well. Your good impression is a fun and cute man, which is in my mind deeply.

Keep you in my mind. Let's meet soon!

Sincerely,
Bella Campbell

Campbell. Imogen's name. Daniel folded the piece of paper and put it in a drawer, then swallowed the rest of his drink. He thought about Bella, but not for long, then turned out the light and got into bed. After a while, it occurred to him he had forgotten to brush his teeth, but no one was perfect, especially him. He slept like a log, dreaming in Chinese—straight through the roosters, the school bells, his phone—and when he woke up, it was already second period. He had slept through his classes, again.

He worked on the roof whenever possible, surveying the river and the mountains, the fields, comforted by the remoteness of where he was stationed. He did not want to go home. If something greater was expected of him, he did not want it—it was not for him—and, really, when it came down to it, why did anyone have to do anything, so long as he placed the burden on himself?

The harp was coming together slowly, and you could see it from the classrooms. Presently, it was no more than a tall, wooden box, the size of a coffin, stood on end. He had sawed, then sanded the sideboards and jointed them seamlessly down the butts and rubbed them with Arowana oil, bought at the market, the same that he used to prepare his food. Against the sky, it looked like a gallows, but he would have it working before long. When he talked about it with his students, they all thought he was crazy. Apparently, so did Guillard.

The man had always been rather full of himself, but since Daniel's return, he had been acting strangely. Like the Canadians, Daniel's motive for moving abroad had been to reach out and learn something from the world, but, like so many others, Guillard only expected the Chinese to reach out and wonder and learn things from him. In departmental meetings, he never contributed—laughing cynically at their proposals instead—and, more recently, he had begun to show up late, red in the cheeks, reeking of booze. Most of the Chinese teachers were alcoholics, so no one on the administration said a word, and in the end, they viewed Guillard as a role model—at least, compared to Connie— unbelievable as that was.

Because of the weather, they had decided to move English Corner into the library, and Guillard had begun to show up more often now despite that little else had changed. On a good day, they would get five to ten students, while on most days, they got none. Guillard would stand next to the window, as if waiting for some- one, biting his nails, and Daniel would sit there, watching him over the top of whatever he was reading, enduring the sound. If stu- dents came by, he would stay. If they did not, he would go. James Li had warned them about this before. It was part of their duties, he maintained, as set forth in their contracts, and they could not leave early—no matter what. As long as the students kept quiet, how- ever, he was not going to find out. Daniel covered for Guillard— not out of friendship but rather a preference to wait alone.

When Bella dropped by, she would never stay for very long, accompanied by her desk mate, and sometimes Flower, eating din- ner out of a small, circular pannikin that had pictures of David Duchovny on the front. She thought he was attractive—more handsome than Daniel—and had decorated the container all by herself, using cutouts from some of the magazines Imogen had brought over with her and later donated among the books. At first, Daniel was uncomfortable with the idea of her talking to Guillard, but they seemed to have made up, and if Guillard had apologized and she had forgiven him, who was he to get involved? He talked to the others and mopped the floors or went down the aisles, orga- nizing the shelves. He had a feeling that Bella was trying to make him jealous, but he could not be certain, nor did he care.

Occasionally, Imogen came to help. Things were not going well between her and Christopher, and she wanted something productive to take her mind off it, to assuage the guilt. Since returning from Changsha, Daniel had been on a mission to catalogue all one thousand books they had collected over the year, and, working alone, it would have taken him most of the winter—probably well into spring. He had his own reasons for wanting to stay busy, even though he would never admit them to himself. They worked for hours, sorting the titles, showing each other the ones they had read as kids.

What Daniel needed to know, more than anything else, was where he was going and how he was going to get there, who he was going to be. He had been thinking a lot about Angela's offer to work at HOPE after finishing the year, but there was something somewhere inside him that said he was not yet ready to leave. He considered mentioning this to Imogen on several occasions, but she seemed to be preoccupied with her thoughts, and in the end, he did not want her to think him feeble. A midyear depression set in. He taught his classes according to a few older lessons that he had been saving for just such a rut and stayed inside, reading and writing, as if somehow that might help. There was nothing to do but work—what kind of life was that? He did his best to stay optimistic, but it was getting harder as time went on. Daniel needed a goal if he was going to be happy, and he needed one fast.

Moreover, Mr. Cai was posing a problem. Along with his son, who studied at the school, he had taken up residence in the library. They slept on the tables, pushing them together, and left their toiletries on the floor. Daniel and Imogen had woken them up the first time they had gone over and found the door locked, and Mr. Cai, like a petulant teenager, had come to the door in a huff, wearing nothing but his briefs. From the hall, they could see a makeshift pallet behind him, as well as the heavy metal shelves and a row of posters, cut from butcher's paper, made by their students on the wall. Where the posters ended were framed quotations by famous authors that Daniel had printed and hung himself. Though the noonday siesta had just started, Mr. Cai looked like he had just gotten up. Standing in front of the door, he asked them why they were there. He must have been somewhere in his forties, but he had the body of a child.

We need to get in here and do some work, Daniel said. We have English Corner later tonight.

The man looked at them and scratched his belly. He had on a faded pair of sandals that were two sizes too small for him. His big toes were protruding over the front, and the nail on one appeared to be missing. Now is not convenient, he said. I am trying to have a rest.

This is the English library, Imogen said. Not your apartment.

Mr. Cai looked at her and frowned. He did not respond.

She's right, Daniel said. The school gave us the room when the year started to use as we see fit. You'll have to find somewhere else—or, at least, let us work in here while you sleep.

Without a word, Mr. Cai closed the door, and, before either of them could react, they heard the sound of the lock click. The two of them stood there, stunned, until finally, out of embarrassment, they started to laugh. Daniel let out his anger on the door, pounding it with his fist.

In the days to come, they worked separately, devoting mornings, afternoons, nights. When he was not sleeping, Mr. Cai locked the door from the outside, but that was about as far as his thoughtfulness went. Inside, the library was a mess. They appealed to James Li, but he would not agree to kick the man out, for he saw no need for what they were doing—the students were busy, and books were books. Daniel could not argue with his first point: since they had set up the room in the fall, only three kids had made use of the system. For the most part, they came to see the foreigners. Still, Daniel had his hopes.

What they learned later on from Mrs. Ou was that Mr. Cai was getting divorced. It was a rare phenomenon in the country-side, but it did happen, and, knowing Mr. Cai and how he acted, neither Daniel nor Imogen was surprised. They felt bad for his son, though, and they tried to be more considerate for his sake. Imogen's parents had split when she was young, and she seemed to lose excitement for the project upon hearing the news. As for Daniel's parents, they had always been happy. They had raised him together, giving him access to every advantage he could have asked for, and although he was grateful, he was also sad. There were no excuses. There never had been.

He thought about this often. Walking back to his apartment one night after eating across the street, he ran into a boy from one of his classes, shooting a basketball in the dusk. As he always did, Daniel stopped to engage him and ask questions, incorporating what they had learned that week in class. He tried a few shots from the top of the key, but none of them went in. The boy was a big one, sporting a moustache, and he had the same name in Chinese as Bruce Lee. Normally, he was a pest, but away from his classmates, he had nothing to prove. They spoke amicably enough. Daniel asked him what his plans were for the upcoming holiday, and the boy started telling him in Chinese. Before he was able to get any-thing out, however, Daniel stopped him. He set the ball on his hip.

Yong yingwen ba, he said.

Li Xiaolong's English was poor, to the point of exhaustion. The rain had begun to fall, and he turned to go in, but Daniel refused to let him leave until he had answered the question. A flash of light-ning appeared and then faded on the horizon.

Family, he said.

With that, he set off running across the courts. Daniel turned, trudged back to his apartment, then mounted the stairs in silence, like a monk. He had not spoken to his own family since well before Christmas. His parents sent him messages, but for some reason, he

never had the motivation to reply. He sloughed off his sneakers at
the top of the stairs, then left them out on the landing to dry. The
note was waiting for him on his door. INVITING YOU, it said.

———

Spring Festival fell on February 7 that year, and to make up for the
time they would miss, the school held classes the weekend before.
Given the unusual nature of the schedule, Daniel decided against
planning a lesson and instead showed the first half of a movie
about American teenagers to his kids. By the start of break, he had
already been on vacation for five days, and he never wanted to see
another scene from that movie again. He knew the exact lines that
his students would find funny and had even begun to find a few of
them funny himself. He played the guitar and did his laundry and
worked in the library, up on the roof. When the rain stopped, he
would go out on his motorcycle, but the rain never stopped.

The Canadians left on a Tuesday and left him their perishables
in a box, departing for Thailand by way of Hong Kong and Vietnam
and Cambodia and Laos. They were still fighting just as much as
before, but they had planned the trip months in advance, and they
were going to rendezvous with another couple they knew from the
program in Siam Reap to tour Angkor Wat. This year, Daniel had
decided to stay in Ningyuan and experience a real Chinese New
Year for himself, since the year before, he had gone to Tokyo to
visit a friend and come back embarrassed by how much he had
drunk. It was the worst time of year to be traveling, and he had no
money, regardless. Spring Festival was the largest annual human
migration on the planet, but not for him. He was perfectly content
to stay at home. The town was more peaceful with no one around.

Bella had invited him to eat at her grandparents' home and
spend New Year's Eve with her family, but so had the carpenter
and his son. He had not committed to either, but still, both were

insisting on his presence. He spent most of the morning lying in bed, then, once he was up, cleaning the apartment. Throughout the day, Bella called to see if he was home and sent him messages. He did not pick up.

As daylight started to wane, he left his apartment and traversed the yard, skirting the puddles that had formed on the blacktop. After nearly three and a half months of rain, the courts were inundated but not unnavigable, and Daniel had to pick his way across them gingerly, like a minesweeper. His shoes were wet, but he did not care. Following Guillard's example, he had learned to line them with old plastic bags, and this made a difference, although he hated to admit it. There was nothing worse than the man when he knew that he was right.

He had a fifth of whiskey that he had brought back from the capital and intended to give to the carpenter as a gift, and he cradled it protectively under one arm as he made his way up to the gate. The air was sharp with the smell of saltpeter. The locals had been lighting firecrackers all afternoon to prevent the loitering of ghosts and, in the process, covered the sidewalk with so much paper you could hardly see the ground. It looked like rose petals had been strewn everywhere. Daniel considered the scene for a moment as the litter scudded along the curb, then coughed and spat and wiped his mouth and looked both ways, crossing the road.

The carpenter's door had been decorated recently. Household gods looked out on the sidewalk with enormous poleaxes and bulging eyes and an air of levity to their bodies that was shown through the hemlines of their robes. The road appeared abandoned, but he could hear the voices of men inside, and he felt his tension begin to ease with the onset of night.

He rapped on the door and waited patiently, turning the bottle in his hands. The whiskey lapped against the glass. He raised one arm to knock again, but before he could, the door opened, revealing the son. He stood there and smiled and considered Daniel with his eyes. His glasses were slanted on the bridge of his nose, but he adjusted them quickly. He seemed to have grown since the last time they had seen each other, but that could not have been more than a matter of weeks.

Xinnian kuaile, Daniel said.

Happy New Year, the boy replied. He moved back from the entrance to let him in and announced to the rest of his family that the foreigner had arrived. A chorus of shouts went up from within. The carpenter came out of the kitchen and offered him a handshake and a fresh pack of cigarettes, then introduced him to the other guests, who stood behind him, shyly looking on. There were wooden desks and wooden chairs and wooden stools about the room, and, in the middle, a wooden table with a hand-carved leaf insert that the man had probably made, too.

Daniel handed over the whiskey after explaining that it was his favorite and went upstairs with the boy to his room, at the insistence of the adults. The interior of the home looked much as it did on the outside—bare concrete and viga holes—and there were no banisters to line the stairway, although the stairs were quite wide. On the way up, Daniel noticed one room that looked like a classroom and went inside to discover that that was exactly what it was. The chalkboard was blank but recently used, and there was a rostrum toward the front.

It is belonging to my mother, the boy said, matter-of-factly, when Daniel asked him what it was. She teaches lessons on the weekend and sometimes after school.

Daniel was embarrassed. Your mother's a teacher? I had no idea. What subject?

English.

Really. Is she your teacher, too?

En.

Kneeling before his bookcase, the boy began to sort through his DVDs. Daniel sat down on the bed next to him, shivering lightly, and hugged his collar into his neck. The boy's belongings required no more than a quarter of the room, but everything had been crowded into one corner, so that the place had the look of a cell. Daniel had known that the woman could speak English, but he had only figured it for a few words. This was the first time he had ever been upstairs in the family's house, and given how long they had known him, it was surprising.

The boy preceded him back down the stairs and showed him to a couch on one of the landings between the first two floors. The space was home to a carpet and a television and a low-set credenza along the wall as well as an oversized picture of the boy and his parents, staged by a photographer, in a field. The boy turned on the television and DVD player as if he had done so at least a thousand times before, then picked out a place for himself on the carpet and adjusted the volume, folding his knees. It was *The Sound of Music*, subtitled in traditional characters, and he seemed to know the lyrics by heart. Most of the dialogue, too. Daniel sat back and watched him, smiling at the boy's fanaticism. Above all else, he wished he could go back to that age, when life was simple and the future was open—back to when it was possible to get so worked up over nothing.

When dinner was ready, they went back downstairs and tried to help lay out the food, but his hosts would have none of it. Daniel engaged the carpenter's mother-in-law in conversation and explained to her how and where he had learned Chinese and offered up a few phrases in the local dialect, which caused her to squeal. She spoke in a slurred, rural accent, which made it hard to understand her, but, fortunately enough, by the time she had finished talking, it was time to eat. From the way her eyes began to wander, he could tell she was not expecting a response, so he helped her up and over to the table and sat down next to her, warming his hands.

The carpenter moved him before they started and sat him beside another family at the other table and distributed the whiskey he had brought among the men present in little flimsy disposable cups. There were no traditions to the meal other than the wonted toasting of the group, and during this, the carpenter focused his time and attention on the man seated to Daniel's left. He was a big, square-faced man of around sixty, and he had the unemotional, stolidly calm disposition of a boss. When the carpenter finished talking, he turned to Daniel. He told him that they were thankful that he had come, then fired off a series of lucky quotes: let riches and treasures come into your house, with the three yang begins prosperity, may all of your dreams come true.

Among the courses were chicken and blood duck and another meat he did not recognize and, at the center of it all, on a serving dish made out of kaolin, a perfectly steamed fish. They toasted and downed the stuff together, displaying the bottoms of their cups when they were through, the Chinese wincing at the taste of the alcohol, claiming that it was *tai tian le, tai tian le*. Too sweet. Daniel took off his hat and scarf, exposing his hair and his ears and his neck, and as he rotated the Susan, he heard the wife of the man next to him whisper something into her husband's ear.

Kan qilai xiang yi ge xiaochou yiyang.

He picked up his chopsticks and picked his way through the bean curd, choosing to ignore her for the moment. He poured another round for the men at his table. Then he poured another round for himself. He was not particularly upset by what she had called him—the people in Ningyuan had been goggling at him for years—but, in spite of that, there was something about the way she had said it that bothered him more than usual. It was more malicious than anything else. Once everyone had served themselves, he got up and, in his best Mandarin, offered a toast to his host in response. The look of surprise on the woman's face was priceless. Daniel smiled. Who's the clown now? he thought.

Her husband commended him for his Chinese and let Daniel pour a third glass for him once he sat down. From the other table, the carpenter stood up, nodding vigorously in support of the man's claim.

Told you his Mandarin was good, didn't I? he said in Chinese.

Fuck! the man said. It's better than mine! Whoever knew a foreigner could speak so well?

They ate and laughed and drank more booze. The man was known as Hong, and by the time they killed the bottle, his face was as red as the name suggested. He owned a lumberyard outside of town and apparently had been supplying the carpenter for years, and, given the way the two of them interacted, Daniel could tell that he had accumulated much more *guanxi* with the carpenter than the carpenter had with him. All of the food at the table was delicious. Daniel asked the group what kind of fish they were eating, but no one seemed to know or, for that matter, care. Hong rotated the Susan, then, from one of the dishes, extracted what looked like a paw.

It was speckled everywhere with a thick, black sauce, but there was no mistaking it for what it was. Smiling mischievously, he placed it on top of the rice in Daniel's bowl. The whole table was watching him. Uncertainly, Daniel prodded it with his utensils.

Shenme ya? he asked.

Gourou, Hong said. Then, with an embarrassed smile, he tried to say it in English. Dog.

The other people at the table nearly exploded when they heard him. He showed no emotion, however, sitting there solemnly, observing the room. The carpenter came over, raving at his English, and, rather insipidly, told the others at the table what they already knew: foreigners don't eat dog. Hong barely acknowledged him. He looked at Daniel and nodded encouragingly. *Chi ba*, he said.

Even though Daniel had been raised in the West, he was not one of those people who considered the consumption of dog a sin. He loved them as much as the next person, but they were still just animals, and the Chinese bred them for their meat. Still, there was something unpalatable about a paw. He tried to explain this to the table, but Hong and the carpenter shook their heads. According to Hong, it was the best part. His expression was so stern and devoid of irony that Daniel could not tell if he was joking, and after a while, he just gave in rather than argue with them more. Both men cheered and clapped him on the shoulder. The carpenter holding up his thumb. Daniel smiled and chewed on the meat slowly, spitting out the bones.

When the meal was over, the carpenter wandered off and turned on the television. He stood there, awkwardly, playing with the remote. Hong's wife and the rest of the men sat around at the table, smoking cigarettes, and while they did, Daniel went to the bathroom and lit one himself, taking a moment to check his phone. There were six unread messages from Bella as well as one from the phone company, wishing him well, as well as another from an 861 area code—Changsha—that he did not know. Opening it up, he saw that it was from Zenith, the girl he had given his number to at HOPE, but it was in no way personal and too long to read—it smacked of a mass text.

When he came out, the others were crowded around the television, like bystanders at an accident. The carpenter was demonstrating his new karaoke system, but no one was singing. The men were all drunk. Drawing closer, Daniel slipped in behind the carpenter and began to read the lyrics on the screen. They were in English, but not familiar, and the video accompanying them was a joke.

When Hong noticed him standing there, he stood up and started pointing—first at Daniel, then at the screen. He pulled him by the forearm to where he had been standing, then gave him a microphone and sat down. *Laowai chang!* he shouted, to the approval of everyone else. Then he started chanting: *Laowai chang! Laowai chang!*

Daniel was not in the mood to sing. He looked at the lyrics and then at the others. They were all studying him expectantly, clapping their hands.

Laowai chang! Laowai chang!

He tried to say no and return the microphone, but Hong had the momentum now, and no one would take it. Slowly, more and more of them started to join in. By the time the song was over, they were chanting insistently like coeds.

Above the sound of the music and the voices, Daniel could hardly make out his phone. Fortunately for him, Bella was not one to hang up prematurely, and he was able to excuse himself justifiably as he exited the room. Outside, a cold blast of air blew down the sidewalk. In Ningyuan, there were no working streetlights in the winter, and other than the one over the gate across the street, Jiuyi Lu was no exception. Daniel raised the phone to his ear, holding it on the windward side of his face. Bella, he said abruptly. You there?

Yes, Teacher Daniel. I'm here.

Sorry. It was a little loud just now.

It doesn't matter. Where are you now? I only called to see if you still might come. We are almost finished eating. You haven't been responding to any of my messages!

Sorry, he said. I haven't been checking my phone. I'm at a friend's house, across the street from Yi Zhong. I was just about to leave, though. Is that OK?

Yes! That's perfect. I will have my grandmother leave you some food. Just drive past *Wuligou*, and you will find it. Mr. Thomas is here, too!

Daniel tried to explain to her that he had already eaten, but before he could, she hung up. Heading back inside, he made his good-byes to the carpenter and his family. His motorcycle was parked outside on the sidewalk, standing obliquely beneath a tree, and as he mounted up, the Chinese crowded together in the doorway, insistent about seeing him off. He waved good-bye and kick-started the engine and revved it and pulled out into the dark, honking twice as he rode past the outbuildings that marked the borders of town. A few fires burned by the roadside, and there were many stars overhead. As he rode, Daniel let go of his troubles, focusing on the land instead. This was why he had moved to China, and he would be damned if he would forget.

The candle flame guttered at the passing of Bella's aunt, casting its light on the pictures behind it. Guillard stood near the door to the hall to the kitchen, listening to Bella, drinking a beer. She had arranged three bowls on the workbench in front of them— one of vegetables, one of meat, one of rice—and she was showing him how to bow and pay his respects properly in veneration of the dead. There was a cup of rice wine on the altar, and after burning a few sheets of joss paper, she poured it out. Guillard studied the unsmiling faces on the wall in front of him. *Ganbei,* he said.

He finished his beer and asked for another. Bella went off down the hall, moping, as she had been doing all evening, then came back and looked at him and handed him the bottle, prying the lid off with her teeth. The rest of her family was in the kitchen, making preparations for dinner, but they still came in routinely to take out the garbage or ask him if he needed anything—especially the aunt.

She was a slender woman, up from Shenzhen, but she flirted with Guillard like she was American, always referring to him as *teacher.* A couple of times, she had asked him how to say something she was doing in English, and he had told her, very slowly, like a parent addressing a child: put on makeup, drink tea, peel garlic, close the door. She repeated the words, laboriously, rolling the sounds in the back of her mouth, then told him how to say them, both in Cantonese and Mandarin, but when she did, there was no slowing down. Bella seemed annoyed by the lack of attention—going in and out of the living room, messaging someone on her phone—but now it was just the two of them. Gimping his way over to the television, Guillard sat down, put up his feet, and took a pull from his beer.

He had almost not come. Although he had resolved things with Bella, the thought of having to face her parents was a different matter. The bruise on her face had healed by that point, and when they arrived at the house, he had been surprised to discover that her family knew nothing. All day, they had been treating him undeservedly, like a guest. Her parents worked in Guangdong, and they had just returned by way of a bus from the high-speed rail station in Chenzhou the previous night, and, as her grandparents were old and never went into town, they were disconnected from the social network of the community. Guillard had kept his mouth shut and smiled, nodding as they talked, but after a while, he had begun to regret the decision. I should have stayed home, he thought.

The only light was the light through the windows, and it gave the room a sort of lunar impression. Bella's grandparents' house lay on a strip of empty road, about half an hour from Yi Zhong, set between two paddies—both fallow at the moment—lining the valley floor. That morning, Bella had taken him out on a tour of the nearby villages and shown him the places she had known as a child, since, for the first hour after he had arrived, he had just sat there, watching the family make dumplings, with nothing to do. Bella had shown him an old temple and an abandoned marketplace as well as both of the schools she had gone to before

Yi Zhong, translating the enormous characters they saw on the walls of the buildings. For the most part, they were advertisements for motorcycles or slogans for the Communist Party or clichéd aphorisms, made famous by Mao. From atop one of the foothills, they had stood and looked out over the construction on the new road to Yongzhou, Bella treading dirt awkwardly, like a stork, in her patent leather shoes. They had followed the headland on their way back, going around the paddies, too tired to talk, bubbles of methane breaking on the surface of the pools, as if the rains had never stopped.

That had been three hours ago, and, since coming back, Guillard had been trying his hardest to get drunk. The living room was about as cold as the inside of a fridge, and there was nothing else to do, but the beer was weak—just like all beer in China—and the only effect it had on him was to make him feel bloated. There was an elaborate piece of Hunanese embroidery on the wall behind him—a large, framed portrait of a peacock with a huge ass, devolving into flowers—and down one side of it, in four characters, a caption written in ink that said something about flowers opening. Guillard was exhausted from the hike earlier and uncomfortable from all of the drinking. He was starting to get hungry. He turned to Bella and tapped her on the shoulder. He asked her when they were going to eat.

I don't know, she said. I can ask my father, if you want. From somewhere behind the house, they heard a long, high-pitched squeal—the sound of a pig getting stuck.

It had been like this all afternoon. Since returning, Bella had hardly been talking, and Guillard could not tell if it was because of something he had said, something he had done. Whatever the reason, she was acting like a brat, and he felt resentful over having been dragged all the way out to the countryside only to be ignored. It was so much like a woman of her, to make him speculate in the dark. He had been trying to chip away at her reticence since the moment they had gotten back, but so far, he was having little success: even the ceremony in front of the altar had been set up by her parents. Presently, she was sitting on the far end of the sofa, playing a game on her phone—a blue, palm-sized device by Lenovo, bedizened with rhinestones, completely incongruous with the room.

Craning around stiffly, he looked up at the embroidery on the wall behind them. The light from the windows reflected on the glass, but not where the characters were. He pointed at it with his bottle. Then he pointed with his chin. What's that say? he asked her. Your shit don't stink in China?

With one eye on the screen of her phone, Bella turned to look up at what he was referring to. Prosperous bloom, she muttered. Then she returned to her game. Guillard sat there for a moment, waiting for her to go on, but, to his annoyance, she did not. He set his bottle on the floor. Then, loudly, he cleared his throat.

Still, she did not look up. The patter of her fingers on the keypad filled the room. Down the hall, a sound of voices came from the kitchen. Guillard frowned and for a brief moment was genuinely upset, but after a while, the feeling passed. Tapping away on the backrest of the sofa, he leaned over and whistled. Still, nothing.

Earth to Bella, he said like a robot. Bella: COME IN.

She looked up at him as though he were crazy. Then she looked back down at her phone and frowned. Once she had exited out of whatever game she had been playing, she put it away in her coat.

Yes, Mr. Thomas? What is it?

What's up with you today? You've hardly spoken since we got back.

She hesitated briefly. I'm sorry if you feel neglected. If you want, we can go back outside.

Guillard smiled. Neglected? Ha, please. Not everything is about me, hon. C'mon, now. You can tell me. What's wrong? Do you feel like I've been ignoring you? I was just trying to be friendly. Your aunt and I, we were just—

No, Bella said, averting her eyes. It's not that.

Well, what is it, then?

She appeared to deliberate over whether or not to tell him. At last, she decided she would. It's Teacher Daniel, she said. All day, he hasn't been responding to my messages. I invited him to dinner, but he doesn't seem interested.

The kid's a punk. What did you expect?

I invited him last year too, but he didn't come then, either.

Guillard took up his beer from where it stood between his legs and shrugged. *Mei banfa,* he said.

There must be something we can do.

What do you mean? If he doesn't want to come, you can't make him. And what is this "we" all about? It's not exactly like I'm dying for him to be here.

Don't say that, Mr. Thomas. You don't like Teacher Daniel?

No, Guillard said, lying. I like him just fine. I only think it's wrong, the way he's been treating you. At the very least, he should respond. He's got an overinflated sense of himself, ya? He thinks everything he does is so special. I'm telling you, that's one of the problems with his generation. The older you get, you'll see: no one's that unique. Hate to say it, but it's the truth.

I don't know, she said. I think that he's quite impressive. He's planning to ride his motorcycle all the way to Mongolia this summer. Did you know that?

Guillard roared with laughter. No, he said. I didn't. It sounded like another one of the boy's harebrained schemes, and he had no doubt that the plan would fall through. The Chinese drove like maniacs, and he had never even seen a road map before in China, and anyways, wasn't it illegal to ride on the freeway? Good luck with that, he said. Bella did not appear to register his sarcasm.

Just at that moment, her aunt entered the room, holding a bowl of sunflower seeds and candy. Setting it down on the table in front of them, she encouraged them to eat. She had on jeans, a pair of slippers, and a dirty apron tied around the waist, as well as a pair of sleeve protectors, frilled at the wrists, to prevent her arms from getting wet. Squinting down into Guillard's bottle, she tried to see how much beer he had left. *Laoshi,* she asked him, boldly, *ni he zui le, hai mei?*

Guillard swirled the dregs at the bottom of his bottle producing a thin, metallic sound. Aside from a handful of the most commonly used expressions, the only Mandarin he knew had to do with picking up women and getting drunk. *Hai mei,* he said. Then, like a customer, he raised the bottle and repeated the words that, by this point, he knew by heart: *Fuwuyuan, zai lai yi ping!*

The woman laughed and told him OK and then shuffled off, waving her hips. She was a scrawny thing, but she knew how to use it to her advantage. When she came back, Guillard thanked her as he took the bottle. Rakishly, he blew her a kiss.

Seriously, though, he said to Bella. It's his loss, not yours. If he doesn't want to come, screw it. We'll have fun on our own.

What do you mean?

Well, we can still have a good time—just the two of us, ya?

She looked at him uncertainly. I am just usually able to convince him—that's all. Teacher Daniel is very shy, I think.

I'm not sure that's the way I'd put it. Aloof is more like it. You know that word?

She did not. He tried his best to explain it, but Bella's mind was somewhere else. After a while, she got up and went into the kitchen, inviting Guillard to come with her if he felt like helping, but he was too tired and cold and bloated and did not feel like getting up.

He watched television and smoked a cigarette. With the departure of the rain, the surrounding countryside was quiet. All he could hear were the sounds of the wok, a smell of food from the kitchen. He cracked a few sunflower seeds in his mouth, but they were completely stale and without taste, and in the end, they did not fill him—only made him hungrier. He put on his jacket and tried to sleep.

In time, he heard the sound of an engine. Half-expecting it to pass, he paid it no mind while he finished his beer, then went to the kitchen to rustle up another and check on the status of the meal. Bella's relatives were hard at work, boiling and chopping and steaming a fish, and when at last he returned to the living room, he discovered Connie, standing—or, perhaps more accurately, slouching—in the door. He smelled of alcohol, to no one's surprise, and had on an ill-fitting, platinum-colored suit. Guillard scanned the yard behind him, but the man seemed to have come on his own. There was a bread van in front of the house—turned halfway onto the gravel, halfway out of the road—and its front had been dented above one of the headlights. The headlights were still on.

The meal was served shortly thereafter on a big circular table in the middle of the room, Bella's aunt rolling the tabletop out from where it stood among the drying meats and bicycles in the hall. They seated him between Bella and her grandfather—a man not much older than Guillard—like some elderly mafioso, facing the door. Connie took a seat across the table from him and started handing out cheap, white-labelled cigarettes to the men, his shirt cuffs casting, then retracting like water sleeves over the food as he did. Bella's family had not invited him, but they made him feel welcome nonetheless. He had gone to the same grade school as Bella's father, Bella's uncles, Bella's cousins, as Bella herself.

Her relatives were a diffident lot, but something about eating together at the table seemed to lighten the mood and open them up. The man on Guillard's left, who Bella told him was her second cousin, once removed, invited him to stand and say a few words, like some sort of blessing, before they ate. Guillard tried to decline, waving his arms, but the family would not let him, flapping their own. In the end, all he was able to manage was HAPPY NEW YEAR, WE ARE FRIENDS, I LIKE CHINA, then, finally, EAT.

Connie proceeded to toast him when they sat down, and throughout the meal, he did not stop. Bella's grandmother, a woman in her sixties with bound feet, watched them quietly and laughed. The food was not bad, but it was not good, either, and after a while, Guillard quit drinking. When Connie asked him why he had stopped, he told him that he was bloated—nothing else—and at this, the man turned and grunted something to Bella's father. Together, they excused themselves from the table.

When they returned, they were pushing a large plastic jerry can between their feet. The container held some kind of liquid, and there were two Chinese characters, penned in Magic Marker, down the front. Eyeing the jug mistrustfully, Guillard turned to Bella and asked her what it was. Across the table from him, Connie was slurring, like some sort of retard, grinning from ear to ear.

Mijiu, Bella told him. A kind of rice wine, made by my dad.

Guillard's face contorted into disgust. Tell them I don't want any. Baijiu is nasty enough, but Chinese moonshine? No, thank you—I'll pass.

Almost reprovingly, she translated this to the two of them, but by that point, they had already started pouring. Connie said something back to her by way of a response, but it was both too fast and too garbled for Guillard to understand. Connie set the glass, with surprising delicacy, on the table in front of him. From a distance, it looked like water, but it smelled like something that had just been thrown up.

Have a try, Bella offered.

Really, *wo bu yao.*

Connie pointed at him and raised his glass, then shouted something in Mandarin. Bella sat there, trying to contain her laughter, but she would not translate what he said.

Tell him I don't drink anything I can't see.

She did as she was told. Her aunt, sitting a few stools down from them, laughed.

This went on for some time, as such scenes often do. The man attempted to appeal to Guillard's sense of pride, but, having out-drunk him once before, Guillard knew that he had nothing to prove. He had zero shame, regardless. He held fast, with his arms crossed, until at last Connie gave up. Bella's uncle, or whatever he was—the one who had asked him to speak at the start—said some-thing across the table, looking to cheer the group up, but Guillard just sat there, picking at his vegetables, unaware of the fact that he was being questioned. At last, Bella spoke.

He wants to know if you are married.

Me? No. At least, not anymore.

For this, the table did not require a translation. The man who had asked him the question said something about Chinese women, and although Guillard could not entirely follow him, he had the feeling that he could guess. It was a fairly standard question: Why don't you find a Chinese wife? Bella started to translate it for him, but before she could, Guillard cut her off. Looking around the table, he grinned. *Shei neng bang wo ma?* Who can help?

There was an immediate roar of approval. Even Bella's grand-father laughed. The Chinese began to talk among themselves as Bella excused herself to go to the bathroom. Guillard tried to fol-low along in her absence, but he could only make out a few words he knew.

Zhangyongbo, women bixugeitajieshaoyixianidelinju, Connie said, mischievously. *Ta wulunsheidouyuanyishangchuang.*

Buxingbuxingbuxing ni huaile, nagenübuxing. Turning to Guillard, the man asked him a question. *Ni bu xihuan nazhong-xiongdawunaode, dui ma?*

Guillard had absolutely no idea what he was saying. Uncertainly, he nodded. *Shi.*

Kanne wo bushigen ni jiangma? Waiguoren duinazhong-juzhiwenyade meinü tebie youpianhao. Birushuo women zijidezhang-xiaomie, he said, indicating Bella's aunt. *Nimen gaichuantongtuile tamen yixia ba.* Once again, he turned his attention to Guillard. *Tamasi laoshi, ni juede zenmeyang?*

Guillard looked at the woman and noticed that she was blushing. Flirtatious as she was, she was not brazen enough to stand up to the rest of the group. Taking that as a good sign, he nodded, but this time, it felt like he was reaching. All of the men, except Connie, proceeded to bang on the table with their fists.

Ta zenmeduizhemekeliande yige waiguo laotounengganxing qu? Connie spat. *Wo guiji ta de lao'ergentadezuotuiyiyangde, yi-dian'r jingshendoumeile!*

Whatever this was, it received a bawdy response, and since Guillard was lost, he sat up, grinning weakly, and laughed along. The conversation went on in this fashion for several minutes, until finally Bella returned. She announced something to the table, and for the first time all night, Guillard could tell that she was excited. As she seated herself next to him, he studied her up and down. Something had changed.

What's got you so happy all of a sudden?

It's Teacher Daniel, she said. I just talked to him.

And?

He is coming after all! Try not to eat too quickly, Mr. Thomas. We don't want to finish before he arrives.

———

Daniel entered to a flurry of acknowledgment, greeting Bella's family in Chinese. As he made his way around the table like a politician, shaking everyone's hand, Guillard eyed him and lit a cigarette. Connie had just distributed another round. He was wearing a mackinaw on top of a sweatshirt as well as a pair of nice leather gloves, and even though it was only misting outside, his legs were soaked from the ride over. As was his hair. Pulling up in front of Guillard, he slapped him on the shoulder, then wished him a Happy New Year in Chinese and sat down next to Bella, removing his coat. Something about his eyes was different—they seemed less guarded, less ready to pass judgment—and after a while, he put it together: Daniel was drunk.

At the sound of his motorcycle, Bella had rushed outside, waiting next to the road with her arms in the air, as if afraid he might pass them by. She and Daniel were currently engaged in conversation, and everyone else at the table sat listening, and despite that he was speaking to her in Chinese, she refused to answer him in anything other than English. Her aunt was fixing him a bowl, disregarding the boy's claims to have already eaten, and in the corner, Connie was pouring him a glass of the rotgut, which, to Guillard's surprise, he accepted. The men cheered him and held up their glasses, then drained them and filled them, drained them again. Connie was shouting something in Guillard's direction. When the boy stood up and answered him, the whole table laughed.

Guillard fixed him with narrow slits, trying to catch his eye. Daniel, however, was not looking at him. No one was. Turning to Bella, he nudged her on the shoulder. What'd he just say? he asked.

Daniel overhead him. Don't worry, he said. All they said is how disappointed they are that you're not drinking. His voice was loose and distant. More confident than usual. Your reputation precedes you, it seems. Connie says you aren't giving him any face.

That's not what I asked her. I want to know what you said.

He told them that even you cannot be drunk all the time, Bella said. Daniel's face went red. Bella seemed to find this hilarious, although why she would consider having an alcoholic for a teacher funny, Guillard could not say. He sat there, looking around at the others. Now that Daniel had been served, the women got up and began to clear away the dishes. Daniel offered to help them, but they insisted that he eat.

Either thanks to a second wind from all of the drinking or an excessive need to be polite, the boy shoveled the contents of his bowl down his throat like a local. The room's focus had shifted onto him, but for the time being, Guillard was not about to try to win it back. Daniel was praising Bella in front of her relatives, and although Guillard could not understand most of what he was saying, he understood it when he told them that she had been one of his better students the year before. Guillard would have expected her to take exception to the qualification, but she did not bat an eye. On the contrary, she appeared to be blushing. He took out another cigarette, lit it off the last one, and spat.

Connie was still badgering him to join them, and eventually, he caved. As he held out his cup, he heard the boy mutter something under his breath.

Guess I was wrong, he said.

Guillard ignored him and downed the shot. The liquor was harsh, but it made him feel better. When Bella's father saw the reaction on his face, he laughed and poured him another, then poured one for Daniel, who thanked him in English, knocking the table with three fingers. Despite such an impatient, rude-looking gesture, the man seemed to respect him for it, lapping it up. Guillard was still trying to wash away the aftertaste in the back of his throat.

Have you been drinking this shit all night? he asked. It's more than likely to blind you.

No. Whiskey earlier. This stuff is pretty brutal, though—I'll give you that.

Guillard's beady little eyes perked right up. Whiskey? Where the hell did you get that?

Changsha.

Damn, boy. Are you trying to tell me that there's been a bottle of whiskey in town since Christmas? You've been holding out on me, haven't you?

Daniel rolled his eyes. Sorry, he said. Guillard could tell that he was not. It was a present for one of my friends.

You gave it to the Chinese? C'mon, now. You know it'll only be wasted on them.

Daniel glared at him. You want whiskey? Go and buy a couple of bottles yourself. Nothing's stopping you. You're the high roller, anyway, if I remember correctly.

I'm not taking any six-hour bus. He turned and pointed at Bella. This one dragged me halfway across God's creation today. It nearly got to the point where I couldn't walk, ya? He swung around to face Connie and Bella's father. *Wo tai lao le,* he said.

The latter toasted him and told him that he was not old, then said that his Chinese was very good. In Mandarin, Bella told them that it was not as good as Teacher Daniel's. They all nodded in agreement.

The boy just sat there, shaking his head. *Nali, nali,* he said.

Learning a new language in your sixties is a whole hell of a lot more difficult than doing it as a kid, Guillard muttered.

Bella looked at him, astounded. You can understand me?

Of course. I mean, c'mon now, you did say both of our names in English.

Actually, Daniel said, we have a saying for that in English: you can't teach an old dog new tricks.

Bella seemed to find this funny. Killing the rest of her rice, she scraped the bones and gristle she had spit out onto the table into her bowl, then balanced her chopsticks on the rim. Always such a young lady, Guillard remarked. Her aunt had come back for the last few plates and stood stacking them, one on top of the other, like a juggler or a clown. Guillard looked at the woman, then at the boy. With his tattoos and piercings and long, stringy hair, he looked like a freak just escaped from the circus. Guillard considered Bella for a moment, and this time, he laughed.

OK. Maybe his Chinese is better than mine, but who's more attractive? Turning to Bella's aunt, he pointed at his chest. *Meinü,* he asked her, *shuai bu shuai?*

Shuai, she responded. Smugly, he leaned back, then extinguished his cigarette and winked at her once. When he turned his attention back to Daniel, however, all the boy did was shrug.

Wo ne? he asked.

Without hesitation, the woman smiled at him and said that he was handsome, too. Other than Guillard, everyone else at the table started laughing.

Well, Daniel said. I suppose that one goes down as a tie.

Guillard frowned, but the woman was already gone. Between additional rounds of mijiu, the men at the table drew additional comparisons between the two of them. In their estimation, Daniel was taller, stronger, and more humorous, while Guillard's only obvious advantage was that he could drink. Neither one of them was especially fat, but that award went to Daniel.

I reckon that's a point for me, Guillard said, mocking the boy. He raised his glass, then set it back down. Here's another one, hon, he said, addressing Bella. Something I've been meaning to ask you now for a while. You've had both of us in the classroom, so tell me, who's the better teacher?

He was being petty, and he knew it—he regretted the question immediately. Bella did not have to think twice.

Why, Teacher Daniel, she said. Of course.

On the other side of her, the boy sat smirking. The liquor had inhibited his senses, and he appeared to be fighting to stay awake. Leaning out over the table, Guillard rapped on it, fiercely, to draw his attention. The cigarettes and lighters jumped upon impact, as if to indicate the arrival of some ghost.

Something you find funny over there? Perhaps you'd be so kind as to share it with the rest of us.

Jesus, the boy said, laughing in spite of himself. Take it easy for a minute, all right? You're going to break the table in half. How can I put this to you, Thomas? You aren't a good teacher. In fact, it's people like you that are ruining this country. I'm not sure if you remember, but you asked me at the beginning of the year what I hate most about China. Well, I think I've got an answer for you: unqualified, lecherous drunks like you, who go around thinking they're entitled to do whatever they want just because they're white. I've got a news flash for you, buddy: this isn't the nineteenth century. You're an anachronism, and an absurd one, at that.

You know, I met an old coworker of yours the last time I was in Changsha. That's right. Jan. According to her, you've never worked at Yali for a single day in your life. He was a kindergarten teacher, Bella. God only knows what else he's been lying about. Hell, I can't believe you'd invite him here after what happened. You might be putting one over on everyone else, Thomas, but you're not fooling me. You've got no right to be teaching children. Foreigners like you make the rest of us look like complete assholes.

No one said a word. Bella sat there with her mouth agape, trying to make sense of what had just happened. She looked at Guillard, then grew embarrassed and looked at the ground. Connie and Bella's father were smoking cigarettes, but they did not seem to have anything to say. The other man, Bella's cousin, was trying to propose some sort of a toast in Chinese. He lifted his cup and said something about friendship, but no one joined him, and after a while, he put it down. Bella's grandfather was the only one who seemed to be unfazed by all of the commotion, but after all that he had been through over the last fifty years, somehow that was not surprising.

Guillard chose his words carefully. You're something else, you know that? Sitting there, drunk as all hell, trying to lecture me on sobriety. If anyone's guilty of being a poor role model here, it's you. How about you take a good, long look in the mirror before you start throwing stones?

It's a holiday, for Christ's sake! I'm not the one who routinely shows up drunk to teach class.

Guillard considered Bella. Then he scowled at the boy. His self-righteousness was about all that he could take. Sure, he had been known to have a beer or two before class, but only to fight off the cold or stave off a hangover or if there was nothing else left in the fridge.

Bella tried to intervene. She said it was bad luck to squabble around New Year's—her word, not his—but Guillard cut her off. He stared the boy down.

You think you're so much better than everyone else, don't you? I can't wait to see where you end up. Idealism can only be used as a crutch for so long, ya? The same goes for being young. I used to be a lot like you, you know. In time, you'll realize—we're not so different, you and I.

The boy snorted, clearing a few strands of hair from his face. Try and scare me all you want, Thomas, but I'm nothing like you.

Teacher Daniel is great, Bella said. You're being unfair! He's probably one of the best teachers I've ever had!

Thanks, Bella, Daniel said. I appreciate that, I do. But for your own sake, stay out of this. There's no reason to get involved.

Guillard stood up and slid back his chair. At the sound of it, everyone at the table jumped. Wake up, he shouted at Bella. He doesn't give a damn about you or anyone else! He thinks that just because he's in China, he's doing something special with his life. You are a novelty to him, he said, turning to face the boy. Isn't that right? Daniel's face paled. He did not respond. After all is said and done, he's here for the exact same reasons as the rest of us: easy living, zero responsibility, and a chance to make himself into whatever he wants.

In the ensuing silence, Guillard sat back down and threw back a shot. The women had emerged from the hallway opposite him, and, with them, a tangible hostility filled the room. Daniel was seated with his arms in his sweatshirt, staring at a spot in the middle of the table, and, when he looked up at Guillard, he almost seemed to be crying.

Fuck you, he said. Then he got up and left the room.

Bella flashed a look at Guillard somewhere between murderous and dejected, then chased after him, flailing her arms. Through the rain, Guillard could hear his engine start, and by the time the sound had abated, the only other person left with him at the table was Bella's grandfather. The old man watched him without expression, then shut his eyes and lowered his head. Behind him, the embroidered portrait of the peacock hung on the wall. For the life of him, Guillard could not remember what it said.

十 一

Winter turned to spring, and the floodwaters receded, exposing the banks, and, where they had, bits of flotsam hung from the branches of the trees, drying in the sun. A new layer of silt had washed down from the mountains and heightened the riverbed along its course, then been laid over with sandbags and dirt and gravel by the caterpillars on shore. Daniel stood on the roof of their dormitory, looking out over the students at play below, studying the garbage in the hair of the willows, the artificial bight being formed. Whereas previously he had always seen local indifference to the environment as quaint, he was beginning to recognize it for what it was: shiftlessness on the part of a town. The wind stirred, mussing his hair, and as it did, the waste-laden tree boughs bobbed along. Like a curtain of whalebone or a sieve or a web or a fisherman's trawl line, set out to dry. Like the gross and shameful bunting of some lesser age of man.

With the departure of the rain, he had been spending more time on the roof, working on the harp or sketching in his notebook, making excuses for what he had done. Since that night in the countryside, he had not reached out to Guillard, and aside from

English Corner, they had not seen each other for nearly two and a half weeks. Daniel stood by everything he had said, but he also felt ashamed, for there was no victory in it, and he had just sat there, mute and unable to come up with anything when Guillard had come back at him. In a way, the man was right. He had no idea what he was doing, and, for all of his idealism, he was lost. If Guillard had convinced him of one thing, however, it was that he was not going to end up like him.

He had barely made it home alive that night, steering his bike through the pouring rain, crashing into the front of the house he had been at earlier, although this much he did not remember. His phone had gone missing at some point, and although the old guard at the entrance had told him that he had come across one, smashed to pieces, under his table the next morning, he assured him there was no way it could have been his, for that person had thrown up everywhere. Daniel had thanked him and offered him a cigarette and made his way discreetly back to his room. He had napped on the couch in the parlor for the rest of the afternoon. When he awoke, his brain was aching. The sun was already down.

He had dreamed of his parents' house and a dog in their garden and the porch he had slept on several summers before. Since moving away to college, he had been without a room whenever he came home, dividing his nights between one of the sofas they had in the basement or that nightmare of an air mattress they kept on the porch. A few times, he had slept in his brother's room, but he did not like having to wake up every morning and make the bed. In any event, he enjoyed the spirit of sleeping outdoors: the sustained hum of crickets, the rustle of creatures in the bush. In his dream, it had been morning, and the dog had been rolling in one of his father's flower beds in the sun, about a foot and a half from where he lay sleeping, with only the screen to keep them apart. In the dream, he had known that the dog belonged to his neighbor, but, in truth, there were no such animals on their block. No such flower beds behind their house. Daniel had met the dog's eyes with his own, then sat up and thrown off the covers and barked, but the dog had just lain there, wagging its tail excitedly, as if unaware of doing wrong. Upon awakening, he had taken a few aspirin and drunk some water and stumbled out onto the balcony in the dark. Across the river, someone was setting off fireworks. The dream had stayed with him for days.

He picked up his saw and resumed where he had left off and did what he could to prevent opening his blisters. It was just past noon, and classes were out until two, but he was finished for the day. Four classes on Monday, one on Tuesday, none on Wednesday. Five apiece the rest of the week. He had English Corner that evening, but he did not feel like going. Recently, no one other than Bella had been showing up, so it was unlikely that he would get in trouble, and, what's more, she only talked about what had happened that night, bashing Thomas, reassuring him that he was right. Daniel did not want to get into it again. He had a phone interview with HOPE at six, and he used that to justify his reasons for skipping. He was not nervous about what they might ask him, but still, he thought, it never hurt to be prepared.

The courts were filled with black-haired students, dribbling, shooting, shouting at friends. Christopher was playing basketball with a few of them, and Daniel watched him from the roof. The guy was athletic. He handled the ball well, and he handled it often, but he never took a shot—choosing instead to facilitate the offense— and in the one or two minutes that Daniel watched him, he made a few beautiful, no-look passes. Once, the kid he was shoveling it to did not see the ball coming, and they had to stop to make sure he was all right before proceeding with the game. For someone so stiff and mirthless off the court, Christopher moved with a certain ease that Daniel found surprising. His students appeared to love him, and Daniel had no idea why, over the course of a year, the two of them had not become better friends.

Moving to Changsha seemed like the logical next step, but when Daniel thought about it, he was still uncertain, and he wanted to be sure. He knew he was not yet ready to return to America. He had been unhappy there for so long, constantly comparing himself to others, but, in a way, was that not what Guillard had accused him of that night, hiding himself away from the rest of the world? Disgusted, he threw down the saw and wiped at his brow, then looked across the river, sucking through his teeth. In the distance, beyond the caterpillars, an army of farmers could be seen plowing the fields. They appeared to be racing, for the soil was ready now, and, after all, Daniel thought, a year's planning began in the spring.

He went down to eat shortly thereafter. As he was negotiating the ladder, he heard Imogen coming up the stairs. She was singing an old, jazzy ballad—carrying groceries, from the sound of it— and when she got to the landing below him, one of the bags ripped and fell on the floor. A moment passed in silence. Then, quietly, she swore.

Daniel went down to find her on her hands and knees, trying to gather the things she had dropped. The landing was covered with vegetables and fruit—a carton of broken eggs—and when she saw him, she glanced down at the mess she had made and frowned in self-pity. Daniel knelt down beside her, picking up a few mango-steens, a dragon fruit, a peach, telling her that, eggs notwithstand-ing, there was no reason to be upset. Everything looked OK. Her skin was tanned from her time in the south, and there were beads woven into her hair. As she sat there, putting away the groceries, they rattled and clicked.

Sorry, she said. I'm having one of those China days. Seems like ever since I got up this morning, nothing's been going right.

I've been there, Daniel said reassuringly. And he had. They packed away the last few items, then rose, sweeping the eggshells with their feet. Here, he said as she reached down for her bags. Let me help you with those.

Thanks. Wanna come in? I'll put on some tea. Chris is out playing basketball with the kids. I could use some company.

Sure.

Got any more classes left?

No. I'm done for the day.

Lucky.

Daniel smiled. I take it you're in a different boat.

Where I am, Danny, there are no boats. She fished through the front of her dress for the keys, then opened the door. I've still got three left this afternoon. Two of them are the worst, and they're scheduled back to back.

Damn, I'm sorry.

It doesn't matter, she said, frowning. Unlocking the inner door, she stepped inside and removed her shoes. I just need a minute to run to the bathroom. Go ahead and make yourself at home.

Daniel followed her into the apartment and followed her example by removing his shoes. He put away the groceries in the kitchen, then, with his hands in his pockets, took a look around the front. The last time he had been in their apartment had been way back at the end of November when they had celebrated Thanksgiving, but since then, they had done little to decorate the rooms. Oddly enough, he noticed, both of the beds appeared to have been slept in. On the counter in the kitchen, there was a jerry-rigged box trap next to the sink as well as a bit of cracker, attached to a chopstick, split down the middle to prop the thing up. The box was weighted with a brick. Daniel paced around the living room, too restless to sit, and inspected the items on the coffee table, the credenza, the television, the shelf. On the pass-through to the kitchen, he discovered a pile of letters. A bulb of garlic, developing shoots. The letters were folded and made out to Imogen. They were all signed the same way:

Sincerely, Your Sister, Bella.

Daniel was reading one of them when Imogen came out, and when she saw him, she smiled. She went into the kitchen and lit the burner. I've got an entire drawer full of those, if you're interested. I've been helping her write a speech.

Daniel grinned and shook his head, telling her that he did, too. He placed the letter back where he had found it. Then, as if addressing a saloonkeeper, he propped his elbows up onto the ledge.

I still haven't heard about your trip, he said. Imogen gave him a halfhearted smile. Did you have a good time?

She turned away and opened the fridge. She did not reply until she turned back.

Not really. It was kind of a disaster, to tell you the truth.

What happened?

Well, for starters, we broke up.

Oh God. I'm sorry.

It's fine. I drowned my sorrows in two-dollar massages on the beach. Things have been pretty bad between us now for a while. I always knew that this year was either going to make us or break us. It's just difficult because now we have to live together for another two and a half months.

I can only imagine. Are you still on good terms, at least?

I'm not that upset. In fact, I'm relieved. You know Christopher, though. He keeps to himself. Since the breakup, it's like he's completely shut down on me. She paused. It just feels like we never really knew each other.

Her voice quavered, and at the sound of it, Daniel looked up. A glaze had settled over Imogen's eyes. Before he could think of what to say, however, the moment passed. She wiped her face. Then, almost as if disgusted, she unpacked the groceries, opening the drawers.

I'm sorry, she said. I didn't want to be like this, I swear.

Daniel shrugged. It's fine. Really.

I just haven't been able to talk about it with anyone since we got back. Somehow, hearing it out loud makes it seem more real, you know?

The water had begun to boil. Daniel stood up and walked around into the kitchen and turned it off and filled up the mugs. Through the window, he could see Christopher in the distance. He was still balling, and he was shirtless—blindingly white compared to his students. A moment passed in which the two of them said nothing. When Imogen turned around, Daniel pointed at the contraption on the counter.

Mice? he asked.

She smiled and nodded, grateful for the change in subject. Only one, she said, but he's huge. We caught him once, a few weeks ago, but he got away while we were trying to move him. He's so bold! He'll come right out when you're in the living room and start going through whatever's on the counter. It's like he's not even afraid of us.

Daniel smiled and handed her the tea. They stood there, sipping out of their mugs in silence.

Really, Imogen said. I'm sorry. I don't want you to feel uncomfortable around us.

Please. There's no need to apologize. I've been through my fair share of breakups in the past, and I know they're not easy.

They went back into the living room and sat on the sofa. They turned on the TV, but nothing was on. Imogen told him more about their trip—the killing fields, the ruins of Angkor Wat, the open-air markets in Luang Prabang—but, in the end, their conversation returned to the breakup. Daniel listened and drank. He did not press her.

Speaking of breakups, Imogen said, how are you? A little bird told me about what happened over New Year's.

I don't know. I'm fine. Thomas is a jerk—that's all. Still, I guess I shouldn't have said anything. I was drunk, and when you think about it, I was picking on a cripple.

I'm sure he deserved it. Wish I could have been there. In one of her letters, Bella seemed worried about you, though. Anything you want to talk about?

No, not really. Thanks. I just need to figure out what I'm going to do with my life. Living here has been one of the most eye-opening experiences ever, but at the same time, lately, I can't help but wonder if it's all just a waste.

Imogen nodded, staring down into her tea, as if therein lay the answer. I've been thinking about that a lot, too, she said. One of my friends just started a company back in Canada, and he's invited a bunch of us to come work for him, but I don't know if that's what I want right now. Christopher, he's going back to work for his parents. He's known that that was what he was supposed to do ever since grade school. It's a lot easier for him.

Any other options?

Not at the moment. I'll figure something out, though. You?

I've got an in with an English training school in Changha. I'm just not sure if I'm cut out for it.

What do you mean? I'd think you're the perfect candidate.

City life, I mean. That and the fact that I'm not really into teaching. Don't get me wrong—it's been great these past two years. I'm just not so sure I can see myself doing it when I'm forty.

How come?

I don't know. I just don't think I'd be happy. Killing his tea, he set down the mug on the table. Who knows? Maybe I'll stay. End up becoming the hermit of Ningyuan. Or maybe I'll try my luck somewhere else. What's Canada like, this time of year?

Imogen frowned at him, playfully. There has to be some kind of job that appeals to you. Don't make it so complicated. When it comes down to it, what do you like doing? Carpentry?

Daniel sighed. No, that's more of just a hobby. Playing music, I guess, but that's not exactly practical.

So? Neither is volunteering in the Chinese countryside. If you're passionate about music, go after it. I've heard you before, and you're good! At the very least, you owe it to yourself to try.

Uncertainly, Daniel nodded. Thanks.

Seriously. I think you should.

The school bell rang, and Imogen smiled at him. Outside, Daniel could hear the students coming in from the courts. She asked him if he wanted more tea, but he told her no, thank you, he had to go. The idea of being there, still talking to her, when Christopher got back was awkward enough.

She walked him to the door, smelling of rose hips and sweat. Daniel lingered for a while on the landing, pacing back and forth after she had wished him good-bye, trying to think of what he could have said to her, for there was much they had left unsaid. Once he had gathered up his courage, he took a deep breath, then knocked again. It felt like it took her forever to answer the door, and when she did, she looked surprised.

Hey, you. Forget something?

He hesitated. Then, without thinking, he blurted out: I think that you should stay. I think we both should.

Her eyes filled with pity. Oh, Danny, she said. That's sweet of you—really, it is—but I've been counting down the days until we're out of here. I can't wait to leave China. I hate it here. I thought that you knew . . .

———

In the weeks to come, Daniel wandered the town, eating his dinners in the square. Niggardly dumplings or knife-cut noodles or skewers of lamb meat—or so he was told. The Uighurs who sold them to him were also seen as foreigners by the Chinese, but they did not enjoy the same privileges as he, and they regarded him sourly as he tried to talk to them, fanning their coals. There was a new fast-food restaurant overlooking the river, and Daniel ate there often—maybe one or two times each week—for there you could get a small order of nuggets and a fried chicken sandwich, all without any bones. The name of the franchise was McConkey's. There was another, right down the street from the temple, that went by the name of KXC.

He befriended two men who owned a music shop across from Yi Zhong and spent an hour there every night. One was a drummer, while the other played erhu, but between the two of them, they could also play the cello, mandolin, guitar, piano, bass. He began to take tae kwon do lessons with his students, befriending the teachers there too, and though they were jocks and not the sort of people he would have been friends with back home, they got along well. Except for two of them, they had been trained in Yongzhou, and one had been the champion of Hunan Province in 2007 and 2008. Whenever they drank, they ended up fighting on the sidewalks or in the restaurants or along the river, in the middle of the street. They appeared to look down on Ningyuan, but perhaps that was part of the reason why they spent so much time with Daniel.

One afternoon, as he was returning home from practice, he ran into Bella on the staircase, descending from his room. She had just put another note on his door and called him to see where he was, and she seemed upset that he had not answered her, whining in a high-pitched child's voice. He had just gone jogging to loosen his muscles, and he was covered in sweat. He was not wearing a shirt. As she told him her reasons for coming, she stood there, eyes affixed to the symbols on his chest.

The annual English competition is next Thursday, Bella said, and I've been put in charge of organizing it. The winner will compete in the provincial finals next month. We were hoping that, as the foreign experts, you, Imogen, and Christopher would be willing to serve as judges. Do you think you can? There will be a talent show, too. Most of the contestants will take part.

She had followed him back to his room. Daniel removed the piece of paper and looked at it. The page had been plastered with glamour shots of Bella, set against various backdrops, including a meadow, a forest, a lake, and there were other stickers too on the frame of the door. Hurriedly, he went through his pockets, looking for his keys.

What about Mr. Thomas? he asked.

Bella made a face. He is not answering. *Li Laoshi* told me that we had to invite him, but I think three should be enough. Last year, there were only two judges, and they were both Chinese. Anyway, she said, Mr. Thomas isn't even a real teacher.

Daniel looked at her but did not say anything. He agreed with her, but neither was he, if they were being honest. How come this is the first I'm hearing about the contest? he asked.

The girl who was in charge of it last year was—how to say?— not very competent. I want to make this year's event special. Teacher Imogen said she will perform a dance at the show. Do you think that you might be able to prepare something, too?

Daniel shifted as he worked on the lock. What did you have in mind?

Maybe you can play a song on your guitar.

I'll think about it. When do you need to know by?

This weekend, if possible.

He told her OK, then unlocked the door. The metal fell to with a clang. She stood there, waiting on the landing. Can I come in? she asked.

I just got home from practice, Bella. I need to take a shower— I'm sweating like a pig.

But we haven't talked in such a long time! I write you letters and call your phone, but you never answer me. Plus, recently, you haven't been going to English Corner. The year is almost over . . .

Inwardly, Daniel sighed. All right, he said. Just give me a minute to go and put on some clothes. Help yourself to whatever you want in the kitchen. I'll be right back.

He left the door open and went down the hall, removing a shirt from the line on the balcony. When he returned, Bella was seated on the love seat in front of the window. The door was closed. Before sitting down, Daniel opened it again.

So, what's up? he asked her impatiently. How have classes been going so far this term?

Bella was browsing the books on his shelves. He had set a bookcase in the middle of the wall, where in most living rooms there would have been a television, and on both sides, there hung an antithetical couplet relating the amount one read to the quality of his or her writing. It had been given to him by a friend. Bella raised one arm, pointing at the scrolls. Do you know what it means? she asked.

Daniel recited the lines in Chinese. Then he recited them in English. Smiling, she told him somewhat patronizingly that his pronunciation was excellent. He told her that he still had a ways to go.

Really, she said, it is almost like you are becoming a real Chinese. My mother and father said the same thing after they met you. If you stay for another year, just imagine how much better it can be.

Daniel shrugged. *Tiantian xiangshang.*

That's right. Every day, make improvements. Maybe one day you could get a job at a large multinational corporation. Wouldn't that be wonderful? That way, you'd never have to leave China!

Daniel nodded, leaning back in his chair. The conversation was proving to require the same effort as a date.

Was there something specific you wanted to talk about? Or did you just want to come by to hang out?

Bella frowned, smoothing out her uniform. I just wanted to see how you were, she said. Last year, you never missed English Corner. These past couple of weeks, however, you have been absent twice! Mr. Thomas isn't very creative—it's so boring when he is in charge. Sometimes, he is not even sober. It's hard for some of the students to understand what it is he's saying. You haven't been sick, have you? You need to be careful this time of year. The seasons are changing . . .

Daniel hesitated before responding. It had always been apparent to him whenever Guillard had been drinking, but he had always assumed, for one reason or another, that the students could not tell. Thinking back on it now, he felt like a fool. They were young, not stupid. He tried to make excuses for the man, saying that it was probably just because he was old or had a Midwestern accent, but then he remembered: he hated Guillard. Why was he trying to protect him?

I'm applying for a job in Changsha, he said. I've had to do a couple of interviews recently. Don't worry, though—they're over. I'll be at English Corner next week.

The moment he finished telling her this, Daniel knew that he should not have said a word. Bella seemed crestfallen, staring at him across the table, and even though he was not inclined to take her seriously, since she had a history of overreacting, he regretted it, for now he had to deal with all of the histrionics involved.

You're leaving? she asked. I thought your plan was to stay here for another year. What happened? Didn't you say that you hate the cities? I remember you telling me that the first day we met.

Daniel did not doubt that she was telling the truth, but he had no recollection of where or when they had met. During his first few days in Ningyuan, everything had been so new to him, including the kids, and students had been approaching him to introduce themselves every chance they got. It was strange now, thinking of her as just another face in the crowd. It was simply time for a change, he said. At this point, nothing was certain. Bella sat there with her arms crossed. It did not seem as though she believed him.

I don't understand. You used to talk about how most foreigners never really get to know China, about how you had a plan to live in the countryside for three years, to get a more genuine understanding. I have always admired you for that. You're so unique. What about that time on *Wenmiao Jie* when we were buying tea and you wrote that *Ningyuan* saved your life? I don't understand how you can change your mind like this, so suddenly. It doesn't make sense.

Sometimes plans change, he said. In fact, more often than not.

But why? There must be a reason.

I don't know, Bella. I need to do something with my life. Over the past two years, I've had fun, but it hasn't really led me anywhere. It's not like I was planning to stay in Ningyuan forever . . .

Bella frowned and looked at her hands. You are a great teacher, she said. The best I have ever had. You've inspired me so much these past two years, and my English has improved because you are here. I look up to you and think, if he can doing it, so can I. As students, we have so much pressure in our lives, but having heard your story, I'm not so scared. You have followed your heart and affected so many students. I wouldn't say that that is nothing!

I'm sorry. You know I didn't mean it like that.

Is this because of what happened with Mr. Thomas? I think you have been acting differently since then. You cannot listen to what he says—he is just a jealous old man.

Trust me, Daniel said. This has nothing to do with Thomas.

Are you sure?

Yes.

Bella scrutinized him. If he was not in *Ningyuan*, do you think you would still be leaving?

I don't know. Who's to say? I told you, though, I'm not leaving—at least, not yet.

It is because of Mr. Thomas, isn't it?

No. It's not. It's just something that I feel the need to do. Like when I quit my job and moved to China. You said you looked up to me for that—well, this is what it looks like, sometimes, following your heart. I suppose Thomas did get me thinking along these lines, but that's not to say I'm leaving because of him. There's more than one angle to all of this, and in the end, all I can do is what I think's right.

She did not seem to be listening. When she looked up, however, Daniel could tell that she had reached some kind of a decision.

I can make Mr. Thomas leave, she said. That way, you can stay here and not have to worry.

Daniel laughed. Yeah? And how exactly do you propose to do that? Thomas has to be one of the most stubborn people I've ever met. He's not just gonna up and leave for no good reason. If he won't listen to me, he's not gonna listen to you. Hell. Why are we even talking about this? Like I told you earlier, this has nothing to do with him, I swear.

Bella looked at the ceiling, avoiding his eyes. If you want Mr. Thomas to leave, I think I know a way how. Like you said, he is not a real teacher. He lied to the school, and there are other things I could tell the principal that are—well, how do you say?—less pardonable.

What do you mean?

Bella looked out the window, as though embarrassed, then stood up and got ready to go. I don't want to say anything right now, but if that is what it takes to keep you here, I will. Please, just think about it, Teacher Daniel. You belong in *Ningyuan*.

From the windows of his classrooms, Guillard had a direct view of the river. The great meander of its body, the farmlands beyond. He stood with his good arm behind his back and the other dangling like a wind sock at his side and the sound of his students at work behind him, scribbling away. The rains had ceased near the end of March and left in their wake a span of good weather that had lasted for weeks and seemed to galvanize his students into, at least at times, paying attention. He taught from the book, despite James Li's warnings, and administered writing exercises often. There were only ten more weeks left until summer, and in his mind, the less work he did, the better.

He turned from the window to look at the time, but if any had passed since last he had checked, the clock had not moved. Guillard strolled up and down the aisle, inspecting his students' papers, doing his best to project the image of someone who actually cared. For the most part, the children were working, but, as always, a few were more interested in sleeping or watching movies on their phones. He did not say anything to them as he passed. Bella had been the most opposed to the lesson, complaining that he was supposed to be teaching oral English, not writing, but, then again, she had been disagreeable about nearly everything since that night in the countryside. They hardly spoke anymore. Before, she had been his go-to whenever he needed a volunteer to answer one of his questions in front of the class, but recently she had been just as quiet as the rest of her classmates, feigning ignorance, shaking her head. At English Corner, she sat with Daniel, and in his absence, she did not stay, but if her intention was to make Guillard feel jealous, she was doing a poor job.

Ten minutes, he announced gruffly, before stepping out into the hall. He removed a cigarette from his pocket and carefully slipped it behind his ear. In anticipation of the bell. Next door, he saw a girl with a scar running down her face eyeing him from where she sat, but she did not smile or otherwise acknowledge him as he winked at her through the bars. He returned back inside and stood at the lectern, making a show of collecting his notes, then looked at the clock and furrowed his eyebrows. Only a minute had passed.

Suddenly, the ceiling began to shake, and his students looked up from what they were doing. Guillard ordered them back to work. Those in the front row did as they were told, but those in the middle and the back did not. Above him, Guillard could hear Daniel and his students playing a game of rhythmic call and response, a method of drawing his students' attention that the boy had instituted at the beginning, middle, and end of every class. The patterns grew trickier as they progressed, until, finally, his students could not keep up. Disgruntled, Guillard unsheathed a mop from where it hung between the bars on the window, then began to rap it against the ceiling. He had trouble reaching it. The only effect this had, however, was to encourage the students seated overhead. They stomped at him in response.

He had broken Daniel over New Year's and seen him infrequently ever since, and there was little he had to say to the boy now, given the way they had left things. Whereas previously Daniel had been smug in his reserve, Guillard's words seemed to have cowed him, proving just how fragile his confidence was. There was a feeling of satisfaction that came with knocking him down a few pegs, for Guillard knew how the boy saw him—the same way as everyone else. The last two months could go by, and he could be completely estranged from the rest. As far as he was concerned, that would be ideal.

Finally, the bell rang. Guillard collected his students' work and went off in search of a place where he could smoke his cigarette in peace. The school day was over, and the hallways were crowded, and though he was jonesing for a bit of alcohol, he had no wish to get caught up in the rush. He stood there and looked out over the central courtyard, on a cantilevered balcony, facing west, the sun on the ridge so gorgeous in its fall, as if that day could be its last.

By the time he finished, the hallways were empty but for two skinny, pockmarked students, mopping the floors. Outside, a gang of laborers was at work constructing a low fieldstone wall in front of the dumpster, as if by hiding it they were being conscientious, which only made Guillard laugh. Currently, they were burning all of the trash they had on hand, while a toxic cloud hung over the school grounds, redolent of cannabis, of dung. As Guillard went by, he covered his nostrils with his shirt, fanning the air with his students' papers, hobbling slowly across the courts. When he reached the pavilion, he folded the sheets in half, then threw them out. A crowd had gathered for English Corner. Daniel had arranged himself on the table, like some sort of sadhu, with both of his legs crossed.

Imogen and Christopher were there too, for it was their night to teach, but Daniel was doing most of the talking, his guitar laid lengthwise across his lap. Bella was sitting in between the Canadians, listening to everything he said, and when she noticed Guillard approach them, she assumed an irritated face. Guillard sniffed at the edge of their circle. While he did not want to join them, he could not pass up an opportunity to rub more salt in the wound. He stood there, listening to Daniel talk. After a while, he interrupted.

Thought you'd stopped coming to these things altogether. What's the word for "malingerer" in Chinese? Looking around at the group, he laughed, but no one answered. Somewhere, someone coughed. He leaned over the side of the pavilion and spat. I'm sure as hell not getting paid enough to teach your share of the lessons, too.

Daniel glanced up but did not reply, then continued talking where he had left off. Bella bowed her head and laughed, amused by the loss of face. Guillard ignored her and entered the circle. One of the students present muttered something under his breath, and this time, everyone laughed. There were two older men whom Guillard did not recognize. One of them was holding a mandolin, the other an electric bass.

Can't say I blame you, he said. He turned to Imogen. There's a whole lot more to look at when this one is around.

From the way the boy flushed, Guillard could tell he had struck a nerve. Christopher stood up from where he was sitting and stepped between them, looking almost embarrassed about it as he did.

Don't talk about her like that, OK, Thomas? Everything's under control here. You don't have to be such an asshole all of the time.

Guillard snorted. Whoa. Easy there, cowboy. I'm not looking for any trouble. All I'm doing is telling it how it is. Even a blind man can see: the kid over there's got a thing for your girl.

Christopher tensed. I think you should leave, he said.

Guillard eyed him, then he looked around the circle. Christopher, Imogen, Daniel, Bella—they were all there, glaring at him with the same expression. Muttering to himself, he backed away from the group, then proceeded down the stairway, using the railing for support. Halfway across the yard, he heard someone call for him to stop.

It was Daniel. He approached Guillard timidly, as if coerced to by someone else. The guitar was slung over his shoulders. He had on a pair of pants that ended midway up his calves that, together with his hair, made him look like a woman, but there was little else about his clothes or the way in which he carried himself that could have been said to be that of a girl. When Guillard saw him, he continued walking, but he could not outpace the boy for long. Soon enough, he caught up.

Jesus, Thomas. Slow down, will you? There's something important I need to talk to you about.

Guillard turned and looked at the tiles. Ya? he said. What's that?

Sorry I've been missing English Corner so much. I'll be better about it, I promise.

Good. While you're at it, it'd be nice if you'd cut it out with all of that banging at the end of class, too. There are other people trying to work here, you know.

The boy nodded and looked at his sneakers. They were green and made of canvas, coming apart at the soles.

Was that it? Guillard asked.

No. There's something else. It's about Bella.

What?

Not here. Will you be home later tonight? I can swing by your apartment after the show.

What show?

There's an English competition tonight in the gymnasium. Bella's emceeing.

Guillard told the boy he already had plans, but that was a lie. Just then, a few children from one of the ground-floor apartments in their dormitory ran past, calling him big uncle something, and laughed. He paid them no mind. Daniel kept talking, stressing over and over again the importance of what he had to say, until, finally, just to get rid of him, Guillard promised to knock once he got back. Daniel regarded him skeptically, then went back to where the others were still gathered underneath the pavilion.

The restaurant next to the gate was practically empty but for its owner and a table full of farmers who goggled at him openly as he sat down to eat. Evaporated wok grease stippled the interior. He had a few beers while he waited for his order, watching the news on TV, then went to the back and served himself rice from out of a pressure cooker in the middle of the floor. The television had been muted, but he could tell more or less what it was about: American warships, somewhere in the South Pacific, encroaching on Chinese waters.

What was it the boy wanted? He ruminated over the possibilities, narrowing them down as he ate. When he was finished, he went down to the river and bought another beer and flirted with the stand's owner, then walked back. The locals had begun to treat him a whole lot better lately, and Guillard was growing bolder about where and when to go out. The road was dark, and, peering into the windows, he realized there was no power. There would be nothing for him to do at home other than go to bed early or get drunk.

By that point, he had quit thinking about Daniel's reasons for wanting to talk with him. Although his experiences did not reflect it, Guillard had always been of a mind that the longer you were able to ignore something, the likelier it was to go away—especially since moving to China. Whereas most men he knew had grown timid in their old age, he had grown more confident, less inhibited, more adventurous, full of faith. More than ever, he believed in himself, and he would be damned if he had to give that up.

He passed under the gate, avoiding the eyes of the guard, and made his way down the ramp at a scuttle, scraping his shoes. The entrance to the gymnasium was packed with students, and from within, he could hear the sound of singing. The gentle strumming of a guitar. Wandering over, he pushed his way through the crowd to get a better look at what was inside, but the lights were off, and it was impossible to see anything. Still, the music played on. He could feel the audience in the darkness, shifting restlessly on the bleachers, and he could see another group of students in front of him, shifting restlessly on the court. After a few minutes, the power came back on, and the crowd started cheering. Daniel was seated onstage, in sunglasses, holding his guitar.

The only other time Guillard had ever been in the building was to watch a game against San Zhong, and there had been hardly anyone there. It was nothing like that now. There had to be at least three thousand students—all of them wearing the same clothes— seated in blocks according to their classes, horsing around. The hoops had been moved to one side of the gymnasium and tied up to discourage spectators from trying to use them, and the markings underfoot were faded so badly that the place had the look of an airplane hangar, not a court. Guillard hobbled down one of the aisles, cradling his beer, and found a place to stand in front of one of the bleachers, ignoring the calls overhead.

Meanwhile, Bella had come out onstage, and although she had a microphone and the spotlight, she was having a hard time getting her schoolmates to quiet down. Running through every language she knew, she waved her arms to call for attention, but the other students merely ignored her and continued talking, Daniel shouting in Chinese. Guillard stood there and watched the scene for a moment, nursing his bottle against the rail, then, without warning, put two of his fingers into his mouth and whistled. That shut the place up.

Bella welcomed the audience and delivered an introduction in Chinese, presenting the judges one by one and curtseying almost all the way down to her knees when she was through. The first act was a student Guillard recognized from one of his classes, reciting a poem by Robert Frost—the one about a man at two roads diverging—and this was met with great applause. The rest of the show was more or less what Guillard had expected—rote memorization, the singing of songs—with the exception of Flower, who, assuming the role of a child orphaned by the earthquake in Chengdu, came out and fell to his knees and started praying, a maudlin appeal to his parents, to God. The judges were all in tears by the time he had finished, and half of the audience was, too. Guillard was preparing to leave when the final act stopped him. It was Bella—the contestant, not the host.

I am going to recite an essay, she said, called "Stuck between a Rock and a Hard Place." The older I get, I am beginning to see the ambiguity in life—it is not so simple, I think, always making the right choice. But that is part of the beauty of being alive! A man once said, "We all make choices, but, in the end, our choices make us." I agree with this wholeheartedly and think it's something everyone should remember. This performance is dedicated to my friend, Teacher Daniel, who has always taught me to follow my heart. At this, a few students whooped, and, shyly, Bella smiled. Then she stepped forward. Thank you, she said. I hope that everyone enjoys.

She looked down at her feet to compose herself, and as she did, Guillard squinted through the darkness at the boy. He was seated at the head of the judges' table, between Christopher and Imogen and James Li, and he was whispering something into the ears of the Canadians, who nodded when they heard what he said. Bella cleared her throat. Then, finally, she began.

Would you steal to feed your family if they were starving? In Les Misérables, a famous book by Victor Hugo, that's exactly what one man, Jean Valjean, must do. Would you befriend an outcast? That's what Huckleberry Finn, a young boy from Missouri, does when he agrees to help Jim, a runaway slave, escape from his master. Would you tell a lie to see that justice is served? How about cheat on a test to come through for those who are counting on you? There's an idiom for these situations in English: "To Be Stuck between a Rock and a Hard Place" means to be faced with two unpleasant choices. How can you decide what to do? In the end, part of you is going to be unhappy. I'm sure that many of you, like me, have had to make such a decision before.

Confucius taught about the importance of altruism, righteousness, and loyalty, but what happens when these three virtues come into conflict? There are many more, besides. No one can give you the solution to your problem—you need to discover it for yourself. These last two years, I have come to realize that knowledge is only a means to an end, not an end itself, and I think that, sometimes, as students, we forget this. When confronted by a difficult choice, there is only one thing you can do: believe in yourself and stick to your values. Perhaps that is not always easy, but it is right!

She went on for another fifteen minutes. Given how tired and preachy the speech was, Guillard had to fight to pay attention. Near the end of it, James Li stood up and tried to catch her eye to cut her off, but this only caused her to start speaking faster. She paced up and down the stage, clopping in her shoes. The other kids began to whisper, and when she finished, it was only to a smattering of applause. She stood there, basking in the light. Guillard assumed the show was over, but apparently it was not.

The acts to follow were varied in nature, and they had nothing to do with speaking English: two boys performing magic, another bouncing miniature basketballs at his feet, a group of three more who came out in street clothes and attempted to break dance, albeit inertly. A girl in makeup, plucking away at an enormous *guzheng*. A troupe of Senior 1s, performing stand-up. From the darkness of the crowd, Guillard watched them, picking his nails, his eyes set on another cast of dancers in particular, their midriffs exposed. Imogen and Christopher sang a song from the Beijing

Olympics, accompanied by James Li, and when they were finished, Bella came back out onstage, leading the applause.

Now, she said, excitedly, Teacher Daniel will play us a song. I am told that he has written it himself. Please, put your hands together!

The auditorium erupted. The boy sprang up from where he was sitting and leapt onto the stage in a single vault. He had a crew of two students to serve for roadies. While they set up behind him, he tested the microphone and bantered with the crowd. The two older men Guillard had seen earlier were with him, tuning their instruments to his guitar.

This oughta be good, Guillard thought. Finishing his beer, he yawned, then rolled the bottle under the bleachers. A boy with a perm hallooed him in passing, but Guillard only stared at him, like a stranger. He did not offer a response.

Once everything was ready, Daniel whispered something into the microphone. A moment passed in silence, then the lights went down. The boy had donned the glasses he had had on earlier, in an effort to look cool, but, given how dark it was inside of the gym, he looked like an idiot. The crowd sat around, waiting for him to begin. During this time, a girl seated somewhere behind Guillard stood up and, shouting loudly, declared her love for the boy. Daniel stepped forward and smiled into the microphone. He told her that he loved her, too.

The mandolin player came in first, picking out the chords with his eyes closed, his shoulders rocking, his hips loose, one foot tapping onstage. Bella shouted from where she stood watching. After a few progressions, Daniel joined him, sliding in slowly on guitar, and performed a tinny, slightly out of tune solo that was off in certain places but had the sound of waking up.

The students cheered at the end of it, as the notes rang out, and once they were quiet again, Daniel began to play the song in earnest. Then the bassline dropped. It was a jaunty, easy rhythm, and, upon hearing it, the Chinese began to rock back and forth and clap. Just by looking at the boy's expression, Guillard could tell it was messing him up. He sang about leaving and broken promises and being jaded by the world and regret, and even though the lyrics had a bit of truth to them, they were—at least, in Guillard's mind—trying to do too much. Somewhere in the middle, there was a solo on the mandolin over the bridge that picked up speed as it drew to a close, vaguely oriental in tone. The crowd roared after the last chord, jumping to their feet, and even Guillard had to admit he would have been hard-pressed to put it down.

He chose not to stay for the awards. The stars were out as he walked back to his apartment, filling the sky like dust. At times, he could hear the sounds of applause behind him. Once back upstairs, he opened a bottle of wine and sat down to drink it, and before he knew it, he was out. It was almost midnight when he came back around. The television was still on, crackling due to poor reception, and moths and mosquitoes hovered outside of his window. Someone was knocking at the door.

At first, he thought it was Bella. He got up and retreated to his room, trying not to make any noise, but once he had had a little more to drink and returned to his senses, he realized that it was Daniel. The boy was insistent, knocking repeatedly, and when at last Guillard answered the door, he wanted to slap him. In one hand, he was holding a letter. Guillard yawned and rubbed his eyes, trying to exaggerate how tired he was.

Calm down, he said. You're getting to be almost as bad as they are, for Christ's sake.

Daniel frowned. I've been sitting around waiting for you all night. I thought you said that you were gonna knock once you got back. There's something important we need to talk about. It can't wait until morning.

Sorry. Must have slipped my mind.

Seriously, Thomas, this isn't a joke. Do you want to come over? Or I can come in. I'm not comfortable talking about it out here. I know we've had our differences, but right now, you have to trust me.

Guillard considered him. All right, he finally said. He put on his slippers and found his keys, then stepped outside onto the landing and closed the door. This better be good, though. I was trying to sleep.

Daniel's apartment was laid out differently than his, with the bathroom toward the front, right when you walked in, and the kitchen overlooking the yard. The whole place had the smell of sandalwood. He ushered Guillard down the hall and into the living room. There was a bouquet of roses beside his guitar and classroom instructions written on kraft paper on the walls and, behind the sofa, a portrait of Mao, from when he was younger, captioned RAISE YOUR HAND and FOLLOW DIRECTIONS. It did not appear as if he owned a television. Guillard stood in front of the sofa, examining the flowers, and when Daniel came over to him, he handed him the note.

You need to read this, he said.

Guillard took the letter and opened it, but he did not inspect it at once. He nodded with his chin in the direction of the bouquet. Who won? he asked.

Flower. It was a unanimous decision. He recited this really moving speech about the death of his parents. Brought me to tears. There wasn't a dry eye in the house.

Those were his parents he was talking about?

Yeah. You were there?

Briefly. How did our Little Miss English feel about losing?

Disappointed, to say the least. But she has other things on her mind right now.

Ya? Like what?

Just read the letter, Thomas. She left it for me this morning. Part of me thought about going directly to the office, but I wanted to hear your side of the story first.

Guillard studied him doubtfully, then considered the letter. It was written poorly, and at first, he did not believe that Bella really could have been the author. He read the accusations slowly, trying his best not to react until it was over, then he read them again. Bella wrote that, on Christmas, she had been invited to his apartment to eat dinner, then engaged in what she referred to as "inappropriate behavior," although she claimed not to have known what she was doing. She wrote that she was going to tell the principal. Once he had finished reading it, Guillard frowned, then he ripped the note in half. Daniel was sitting on the arm of the sofa across from him, scrutinizing him closely, like a hawk.

Is it true? he asked.

Of course not. I've never touched her before in my life. Leaning back, he rubbed his forehead. She did come over to my place that night, while the rest of you were away in Changsha, but it was her idea, not mine. I couldn't get rid of her, ya?

Really?

C'mon, kid. You know how she is. Guillard sat back and knit his hands across the back of his head and looked up, staring at the ceiling. You got anything to drink?

The boy was still trying to decide whether or not to believe him. He stood up and went into the kitchen, poking around in one of the cupboards under the sink.

Gin OK?

Not by itself.

Daniel made him something simple that was red and tasted like cough syrup. He came back stirring the drink with a chopstick. He was eyeing Guillard just as uncertainly as before.

Guillard took the glass and downed it without thinking. It was not good, but after a year of drinking baijiu, it wasn't bad.

Why are you showing me this? he asked.

Daniel sighed. Like I said, I wanted to hear your side of the story first. If word of this gets out, things are going to turn really sour, really fast. After what happened before, I know I don't have to tell you. Also, to be honest, I'm not sure I trust Bella. She's been acting strangely these past few weeks. I didn't think I'd believe you, but, God help me, I do. I don't know how you're going to get out of this, but if you want to avoid a mob, you better act quickly.

By doing what? It's basically her word against mine, ya?

You need to get out of Ningyuan. At this point, I don't think there's any stopping her from going to the school. She seemed pretty adamant about it the last time we talked.

When was that?

Earlier tonight. I stopped her after the show, but she wouldn't listen to anything I had to say.

Fuck that. Like I said before, I didn't touch her. I'm not about to leave at the drop of a hat just because Bella's upset I was mean to you. Let's be honest, that's what's going on here. If you can agree to vouch for me, what's the worst that can happen? Bella has no way to prove anything. She's just a kid.

Daniel sat there, shaking his head. I'll give you the benefit of the doubt, Thomas, but it ends there. Maybe you're telling the truth and you didn't do anything, but I wasn't here. I'm not taking sides. I'll give you a ride to the station in the morning, if you want, but other than that, you're on your own. Just know that, if I were in a similar situation, I wouldn't be taking any chances.

Guillard sucked at the ice that was left at the bottom of his glass. Ya, he said, I bet you wouldn't. Only a guilty man runs. I'll try to find Bella tomorrow and talk some sense into her. I know exactly what she wants: an apology, maybe some attention. Trust me, by the weekend, all of this will have blown over.

Did you hear what I just said? You need to leave, Thomas. As soon as possible. If news of this spreads, it has the potential to be very bad. Not just for you, but for all of us. I, for one, enjoy being able to go out at night. Bella doesn't wanna talk to you, and given everything that's happened, I don't think it's a good idea for you to be going anywhere near her.

Guillard sat there, staring at him. Are you done?

No. You need to consider this more carefully. I've talked to Bella, and I'm telling you, she's on a witch hunt. Do you really want to end up going to jail in China?

Guillard set down his glass. I'm going to bed, he announced. Why don't you just worry about yourself. Seems to me that's what you've always been best at, ya? I'll handle it from here.

十三

That gaudy star set low on the horizon, bleeding of its color on the jagged karst below. Daniel sat on the roof of their building, surrounded by tools, picking out the melody to a song he had written earlier, about a lost and wandering soul. The harp stood before him—not yet completed, but getting close—and as he sat there, plucking away at his guitar, the wind began to stir.

The harp groaned. He had installed the strings and tuned them that afternoon, but still they sounded nothing like what he had imagined. Instead of a high, ethereal tinkling, all that came out was a low, resonant drone. If he could, he would fix it later. For now, he had done enough for one day. The sky was ablaze, and the shadows were advancing, sliding down from the mountains across the fields, and the lights in the houses across the river had started to flicker against the hills. He took out his cigarettes and lit one and smoked it and, when he was finished, stubbed it out on the roof. He was starting to find the habit more and more disgusting, but sometimes, he reflected, you just had to learn certain things for yourself.

It was the Fourth of July, which also happened to be his birthday, but he had not told anyone, and no one knew. Bella was in Beijing, traveling with her relatives, and she would not be back until the middle of the month. The Canadians had left that morning, seen off by their liaison and other handlers in the yard, Christopher schlepping their suitcases down from their room, Imogen watching him while she stood by. Daniel had never seen her so happy before, and apparently he was the only one who knew they had broken up. The principal kept asking them when they were going to have kids.

Mr. Cai had been appointed to drive them—he had just earned his license earlier that week—but he did not say anything to them as he loaded their bags, muttering under his breath. They had finally convinced James Li to evict him from the library, and he had neither forgotten this nor come to forgive them since. Daniel had offered to help him with Imogen's bag but had been immediately rebuffed. You are too cruel, the man had shouted at him. Too cruel, yes!

They had made their good-byes in front of the van and promised to keep in touch once they were back, but all three of them knew this was not going to happen. Mr. Cai had been impatient to get underway and sat there smoking up front, turning around to harry them through the window every so often. He had on a pair of fingerless leather gloves. Mrs. Ou started crying when it came her turn to say good-bye, and to the surprise of everyone else, when Imogen saw her, she did, too. Hugging the woman, she told her to take care, then turned to Daniel. It took her a moment to compose herself.

Bye, Danny, she said. I'm going to miss you. You better call us next year. I mean it!

Don't worry, he said. I will. Have a safe trip back.

She smiled. Daniel shook Christopher's hand, then opened the door for them and stepped aside. Imogen climbed in first, taking the front row for herself. She rolled down the window and waved good-bye to them. Daniel lifted one arm in response.

Let me know if you ever find out what happened to Thomas. I have a feeling he's still out there somewhere, drifting around.

Hao.

Good luck to you, Danny.

Thanks. You, too.

With that, the van pulled out and trundled across the yard and passed beneath the entrance, then they were gone. As the dust settled, the others dispersed, and Daniel went out to buy some breakfast, run a few errands, visit the temple, wander, get lost.

Only a guilty man runs. Guillard had disappeared the day after the English contest without informing anyone—not even Daniel—of his plans. Even though this had been his advice to him, he could not help but feel at fault, for it seemed as though the man had fooled him by playing it so casually. Since then, his words had been ringing in his head. Daniel certainly had no love for Guillard, but doing the things he had been accused of required a certain level of evil, which, in the end, he did not think the man possessed. Nevertheless, there was plenty of room for doubt. He felt bad about lying to the others, but he was afraid of what they might think of him if they found out the truth. He and the Canadians had been asked to teach Guillard's students for the rest of the term, on top of their own classes, and it had been a miserable couple of months.

Now, however, he was alone. Classes were out until September. He had decided to stay for the summer, foregoing his usual trip home, but, after that, who knew? If there was one thing he hated about China, it was the way it was constantly trying to imitate the West, and he had realized that Changsha was too much of a reminder of this for him to move there. He had not come for a good time. He was seeking self-improvement.

The sky was still light when he climbed down into the stairwell, but the yard was completely deserted. As he made his way out to the street, he thought about where he was going to eat. For the last two years, he had been dining at the same small family-run restaurant across from the gate, and although he was friendly with the owner and his children, he felt like trying somewhere else. Furtively, he snuck past the guards, hoping to avoid being seen, but before he was able to make it out of sight of the restaurant, Mrs. Ou called his name.

She was standing across the street. She was holding an envelope in one hand, and she was waving it over her head like a semaphore. Daniel stopped and smiled, hailing her back, then turned around to look at the chef, who by that point was staring at him, too. Excitedly, Mrs. Ou came over, gawking at him shamelessly, as if she had never seen a foreigner before, and Daniel allowed her a few moments to ooh and aah and drink him in. She had not seen him since that morning, and since that morning, much had changed.

Daniel, she shouted. You look like a monk!

Running one hand through his hair—or what was left of it—he smiled. Thanks, he said, I guess. *Ni xi bu xihuan?*

Xihuan. It is more handsome, I think. Before, when it was longer, you looked like a woman.

He smiled at her bluntness. Trying to shift the attention away from himself, he looked down and pointed at the envelope. On the back, it bore the insignia of his former program.

Shenme dongxi? he asked.

Mrs. Ou smiled at him conspiratorially. He still could not get over how big her teeth were. Glancing behind her, as if what she was about to do was illegal, she loosened the tie from around the button, then opened the envelope and passed it across.

Next year's teachers, she said. Go ahead, have a look.

The envelope was filled with forms and photocopies and pictures of the incoming volunteers as well as essays about why they wished to move abroad. Daniel riffled through the documents.

There was a hollow-eyed boy from Michigan and an older woman from New York and a girl from California named Hannah Morrow who had long black hair and was perhaps the most beautiful thing Daniel had ever seen. Mrs. Ou smiled at him as he looked at her picture, but when he noticed her watching him, he put it back. She asked if he had eaten dinner yet, and despite that he had not, he told her yes. This appeared to satisfy her. Reorganizing the documents, she placed them back inside the envelope, then set off.

He crossed the river and turned at the rotary and followed the road past the International Hotel, eventually discovering an open-air restaurant across from the station that specialized in fried oysters and pig's feet, sold as food. There was a boy in an oversized guard's uniform in front of the station who looked up at him as he sat down and a table full of men who were drinking baijiu, their shirts rolled up onto their stomachs to stay cool. He sat and read while he waited for his meal, drinking a beer in the orange light, and at one point, a car pulled up beside him with a man hanging out the window who was either an idiot or a drunk. He could smell the wet hair from the salons across the street, and when the waiter delivered his food, he wanted to know where he was from. *Meiguo,* Daniel told him, laying down his book, and when the man heard this, he smiled, submitting his approval in the form of a thumbs up. Whether this was made in reference to Daniel's Mandarin or country of origin, who knew. Maybe both. He returned the gesture in kind. Then, so as to discourage the man from lingering, he picked up his book and started to eat.

He read and smoked and wrote in his journal, killing another beer in the process. He felt happy with his decision to stay but also restless and unsure of his prospects, for another year had passed, and during that time, he had come no closer to figuring out what it was that he wanted out of life than he had been when it had started. By and by, he came to thinking about his friends. He had lost touch with so many of them since graduating from college, and only one had remembered to call on his birthday, but he did not blame them—he blamed himself—for he was equally at fault. What more could he expect? If you went away for so long, others were bound to forget you. In the end, when he thought about it, he had gotten exactly what he wanted. Had he not?

He finished his oysters and continued reading. A woman had made herself comfortable at the table next to him, but she was not eating anything—at least, not as far as he could tell. She was talking on the phone. Without meaning to, he overheard a bit of her conversation, and to his surprise, it was in English, although what she was saying did not make sense. Glancing over at her, he caught her eye, and when the woman saw him, she smiled.

Blushing slightly, he turned away, burying his head in his book. The woman continued to prattle, as though talking to a child, and the more he listened, the more he felt confident that she was talking to no one, in truth. A few moments passed, and nothing happened, until, at last, the table shook. Someone had seated herself across from him, and, feeling uncomfortable, he lowered his book.

To his relief, it was not the woman, but a girl who looked to be about his age, surrounded by friends. From the way she lay sprawled across the table, he could tell she was very drunk. Her friends were all trying to make her get up, apologizing to Daniel in Chinese, but after a few minutes, it became clear that they would not be going anywhere until she was ready. Eventually, they gave up.

Hai hao ma? Daniel asked.

The girl groaned and told him that she was fine, then, raising her head from the table, offered him a bleary-eyed look. Belligerently, she asked him how he was able to read and eat at the same time. One of her friends leaned down and, smiling, explained to her that Daniel was a foreigner, but still she did not seem to understand what this meant. She continued to badger him in Mandarin. She asked him why he had come to China and, more pointedly, what he was doing in Ningyuan. Daniel told her that he was bored of America, and when he spoke, the others started, taken aback. They considered him as if he were crazy. Daniel asked the girl if it was her birthday, and again she nodded. Then, suddenly, she threw up.

One of her friends spoke a little English, and while they were cleaning her up, he asked Daniel questions and told him what they had been doing that night and suggested that he join them, praising his Chinese. He was just as drunk as the rest of them, but in listening to him talk, Daniel could tell that there was a frantic, overstimulated energy to the way in which he conducted himself that was not the result of any drug. Up until then, they had been singing KTV at the International Hotel, and they were going to meet up with some friends who were at a nightclub once the girl was back on her feet. He worked across the river at a toy factory and was originally from Dengzhou, and he had met the Canadians once in a restaurant. His English name was Boy.

Nali a? Daniel asked. To his knowledge, there were no nightclubs in Ningyuan.

To disco, Boy responded. In English this time. *Zanmen qu disco yiqi wan ba.*

Daniel looked at him as if he did not understand. *Xing,* he finally said. You lead the way!

He paid for his oysters and followed the others and accepted a cigarette from one of Boy's friends. The girl, whose name was Li Hua, had just turned twenty-four—the same age as Daniel—but Daniel did not make any mention of this, for the Chinese were already treating him as if they knew. They stumbled back across town and turned at the river and headed for the square, laughing and yelling and pulling down their pants to piss on the sidewalk, beneath the light of a gibbous moon.

They came to a building across from the Confucian temple that, in the two years Daniel had spent working in Ningyuan, he had passed many times before. In through an unmarked door, up a flight of narrow stairs, down an unlit hallway that was crowded with washing, tenants eyeing them as they passed. Daniel could hear the muted thumping of an electronic bass overhead, and after ascending another flight of stairs, they came to a door covered in rubber flaps. Boy pushed aside the curtain, encouraging Daniel to enter, then stubbed out his cigarette and spat on the floor and waved the rest of them through.

The room was dark and loud and smoky, and there was a girl in fishnet stockings on stage. Neon-green laser beams filled the air. By the time Daniel's eyes had adjusted, Boy and the others were already halfway across the room, and he had to push his way through the crowd in order to catch up with them. On the other side, there were tables and chairs against the wall and, at one of them, a bewildered-looking child who seemed barely old enough to walk, accompanied by adults. Boy called Daniel over to where he was standing and introduced him to a booth full of men, then offered him a drink and a slice of watermelon, then went off to dance. Daniel attempted to make conversation, but he could not hear anything over the music. He looked around the table. Li Hua was already passed out on the bench.

When the music died down, the DJ made an announcement, urging the crowd to welcome the next act—a pair of sisters, in town for two nights only, all the way from Bangkok. The men at their table roared and got up, pushing their way toward the stage, pulling Daniel along after them. Laughing hysterically, like kids. A sweaty Boy stood next to one of the loudspeakers, and when he saw Daniel, he grinned. Is it true? Daniel asked him. Are these women really from Thailand?

Ladies, Boy said, by way of correction. *Renyao*. Look. See!

Whatever Daniel had been expecting, it was not this. A pair of kathoeys in elaborate showgirl regalia emerged on stage and began to enact some sort of a bawdy cabaret. Gaunt jawlines. Volute brassieres. Feathers of many different colors, sprouting from their heads. He turned to find the audience laughing at the dancers, shouting insults in Chinese, and as one of them stepped forward to kick her leg above her head, a man in the front row reached out and grabbed it, causing her to fall.

Freaks, Boy shouted in English. I hate the fucking gays!

Daniel needed to get some air. Whether because of the smoke or the beer or the oysters or the attitude that was now general inside the bar, he felt nauseous and ready to vomit, suddenly light-headed, unaware of where he was. He went to the bathroom and squatted over a toilet and attempted to purge himself, but he could not. The air was cool, but it reeked of urine. You did not miss this, he thought.

He went back out and stood in the doorway, watching the locals continue to jeer. A man from the audience had been called up onstage and seated in one of two armless chairs, and the trans-vestites were prowling the length of the dance floor, searching for another to join him. Before he could be seen, Daniel ducked out the rear, but as he was leaving, he ran into one of his students—a girl from Bella's class—smoking in the hall.

What're you doing here? he asked. From the way the girl looked at him, it seemed as though she was wondering the same thing. She offered him a cigarette. Thanks, he told her, but no.

By the time he got home, all he wanted to do was sleep. He lay in bed, staring at the ceiling, thinking about the year to come. The wind blew occasionally outside of his window, and every time it did, the harp groaned. After a while, he gave up trying to sleep and found his cigarettes in the dark. Dragging his feet, he navigated his way down the hallway in his boxers and went out onto the balcony to have a smoke.

The yard was quiet aside from the frogs, and there were a few bats hunting for mosquitoes beneath the eaves of the building next door. Looking up at the moon, Daniel thought about his family, and for the first time in about as long as he could remember, he missed home. The wind blew, and the harp groaned, blaring its warning across the yard, and across the river, the lights in the farmhouses appeared to gutter, like exhausted suns, fallen to earth.

Epilogue

He stood on the curb outside of arrivals, searching for the metro rail, the Siamese smiling at him in the way of hosts, always eager to please. It had taken him over an hour to pass through immigration, and that was only after having to walk what seemed like the entire length of the airport on foot. Suvarnabhumi was loud and busy, yet modern, and the AC was broken—just his luck—but by the time he had collected his belongings, he had been ready to call it a night. He had followed the signage correctly, he thought, but still somehow managed to end up in the wrong place. After a while, he gave up. Hailing a cab, he paid the driver using the last of his money, then climbed into the backseat and nodded off, dreaming of Bangkok. He knew that he would have a drink in his hand soon enough, and, after all, he had always been a believer in second chances.

Acknowledgments

The author would like to thank Bailey Carroll, for humoring his storytelling at a young age and being the best sister a guy could ask for; Marion Benjamin, for raising him into the man he is today; Sean Freund and Vincent Pueraro, for giving him a bed and a job and a visa when he needed it most; Margaret Wu, for her love; Ruggero Bozotti, for inspiring him to write; and, finally, Mandy Au Yeung, for being the best example of what it means to be a good person, every day.

About the Author

Quincy Carroll was born and raised in Natick, Massachusetts. After graduating from Yale in 2007, he moved to Hunan, China, to teach English. Upon returning to the States, he was a student in the MFA Creative Writing program at Emerson College. He currently teaches Mandarin in Oakland, California. This is his first novel.

List of Patrons

This book was made possible in part by the following grand patrons who preordered the book on Inkshares.com. Thank you.

Adams P. Carroll
Albert C. Turn
Alexander Galimberti
Allison Brooke
Ani Tajirian
Bailey Carroll
Benjamin Jones Kaufman
Benjamin Yuen
Bill and Susan Fink
Callie Crossley
Carly Strang
Christopher Hathaway
Christopher V. Cronin
Diane Young-Spitzer
Frederick Tajirian
Geoffrey Bernstein
Glenda Manzi
Huang Lei
Jamie and Caroline Sturm

Janet Wu
Jason Lacerna
Jian Gao
Jia Zhai
John W. Cochrane III
Kat Deutsch
Kristen Kelch
Mandy Au Yeung
Mei Ling Krebsbach
Michael John McKee
Nicholas Adams-Cohen and Beidi
   Zhang
Nicholas E. Spiro
Oliver C. Davies
Ruggero Bozotti
Sean Freund
Vincent and Millie Au Yeung
Vrej V. Tajirian

Inkshares

Inkshares is a crowdfunded book publisher. We democratize publishing by having readers select the books we publish—we edit, design, print, distribute, and market any book that meets a pre-order threshold.

Interested in making a book idea come to life? Visit inkshares.com to find new book projects or to start your own.